*Their stand for truth...*

*could cost them their future.*

# Impasse

# Portraits

*The Balcony*

*Blind Faith*

*Endangered*

*Entangled*

*Framed*

*Gentle Touch*

*Heaven's Song*

*Impasse*

*Masquerade*

*Montclair*

*Morningsong*

*Shroud of Silence*

*Stillpoint*

*Walker's Point*

9709

# Impasse

LAUREL OKE LOGAN

BETHANY HOUSE PUBLISHERS
MINNEAPOLIS, MINNESOTA 55438

*Impasse*


Published by Bethany House Publishers
A Ministry of Bethany Fellowship, Inc.
11300 Hampshire Avenue South
Minneapolis, Minnesota 55438

Printed in the United States of America.

**Library of Congress Cataloging-in-Publication Data**

Logan, Laurel Oke.
Impasse / by Laurel Oke Logan.
p. cm. — (Portraits)
ISBN 1-55661-976-6
I. Title. II. Series: Portraits (Minneapolis, Minn.)
PR9199.3.L636147 1997
813'.54—dc21 97-33834
CIP

More so than any other writing project I have previously taken on, this book is a product that each of my children has contributed to. I wish to express, with all my heart, my thanks to each of them.

To Nate (11), who was so faithful in asking how the book was coming along and who always had an encouraging word to say;

to Jessica (9), who plans to be a writer herself someday and who finds such joy in writing and reading—anything and everything;

to Jackie (7), who took care of me while I was tucked away in the office writing, bringing me anything I might need even before I asked;

and to Alex (6), who reminded me with his pure boyish exuberance that success in life comes not so much in the big things we try to accomplish, but in how much joy we gather daily.

To each of you, I want you to know that I'm grateful for every day we share.

LAUREL OKE LOGAN is the author of the bestselling *Janette Oke: A Heart for the Prairie* and *In the Quiet of This Moment*. Her first novel, *Gillian*, is part of the SPRINGSONG BOOKS for teen readers. Laurel and her husband make their home in Indiana with their three children.

# One

*Friday, January 1, 1999*

With the edge of a freshly polished fingernail, Esther Branson traced the rim of her water glass, then dunked the lone piece of ice floating there. Switching the receiver to the other ear, she forced a long, controlled breath. The telephone was ringing, unanswered, for a third time.

Annie might not be at home. Leaning back against the kitchen counter, Esther prepared herself for disappointment.

"Hello?"

"Annie! You're home. Are you sitting down?"

"Oooh. Good news, I hope."

"The best. It happened, Annie. Last night, he asked me."

"Asked you what?" But Esther knew that Annie understood.

A quick glance down at the engagement ring that glittered on her slender hand brought a girlish laugh to Esther's voice. "*The* question. He loves me and he wants me to—"

"Stop," Annie cut in. "I get the idea. But what did *you* say?"

"Well . . . yes, of course. I said yes."

Silence followed.

"Annie, are you there?"

"You know I am." The words rattled dryly through the telephone wires.

"Well, say something. What do you think? Aren't you excited? Talk to me."

"I can be honest? Really honest?"

"When have I ever been able to stop you?"

Annie's voice was gentler now. "He's not the one, Esther. He's not right for you. You're too good for him."

Esther's laugh sparkled back through the phone line. "Too good for Neal Parker? Too good for a handsome, successful, well-respected businessman? Too good for the man who saved my career and gave me my first real chance to succeed?"

"You don't owe him anything." There was a deliberate sting in her words.

"That's not the point. I love him, Annie."

"You only *think* you do."

Silently, Esther swallowed the anger and betrayal rising inside her before trusting herself to speak. She should have known Annie would react this way, but she had been overcome with her own excitement. "I do love him. I'm old enough to know what I want, and I do love him. I'm sorry you won't share this with me, but that doesn't change anything. I'm going to marry him, Annie. And I'd hoped you'd be more supportive. We've been friends a long time."

"Long enough for me to want only the very best for you." Annie's voice had softened again.

Esther was still ruffled. "That's easy to say from your cozy status. You're already married and settled. I want a chance to be happy, too, Annie. I'm tired of being alone."

"Loneliness is better than regret."

"But happiness is—"

"Hard to find," Annie cut in. "You don't need *him* to be happy. You're perfect just the way you are, Esther! You're young and smart and very beautiful and talented and great to be around. You've got a career that's significant and—"

"Stop it, Annie."

"It's true!"

Esther leaned against the kitchen doorway and sighed.

Annie paused, too. "It's not the fifties anymore. You've got a career. You don't need to *marry* someone successful. You *are* someone successful!"

"You can say that because you've already got Max."

"Well, you've still got me."

"Yeah, you're great. But I want more than that. I want someone here—someone who loves me."

"Get a dog."

Esther couldn't keep back the chuckle that Annie always seemed to be able to coax from her.

"Listen," Annie went on. "I'll give him a chance. I'll do my best to like him. Just promise me one thing. Be very careful, Esther. Give yourself a long engagement and don't take any step forward in the relationship until you're very sure."

"Isn't it a little late for that? I'm pretty committed already."

"No way! Until you let him put that wedding band on your finger, you're still single. This is for keeps. Take your time."

"You know me—I'm nothing if not careful."

There didn't seem to be much more to say. Esther made a vague attempt at small talk but was more than anxious to end the conversation and have some time to contemplate Annie's reaction. Surely Annie wasn't right. Well, she would be careful. She would proceed slowly.

And he would understand. She was certain.

# Two

*Thursday, February 18*

The hollow slam of a locker door reverberated through the empty hallway, followed by the shuffle of feet and papers as the last students straggled out. An exaggerated silence remained. To Jon Shepherd, a veteran teacher of almost eleven years, it was an all-too-familiar silence. There had been so many days when it had fallen as a welcome relief, but today Jon could not enjoy the after-school stillness. The ache in his own heart now made him wonder if he had ever truly found comfort in the quiet. Oh, he had laughed with the other teachers about silence being "golden," but, at the same time, he knew that if he'd been born to do anything, it was to teach. Now his future seemed to hold nothing but questions as he tried to picture how he would fill his days away from the hum of activity at the junior high school in suburban Atlanta.

Slumping down in his chair, he let his head rest against its cool wooden back and tried to sort out his tangled thoughts. Two large boxes filled with his own teaching materials and books were waiting on a first-row table. His mind rummaged through the jumbled contents of his boxes, wondering what might still be left to pack up, but disappointment and uncertainty kept stealing his ability to think.

Then, from far down the hallway, the sound of approaching feet interrupted his mental wrestling match. Jon stood and tucked the last of his supplies into the boxes. He presumed the visitor would be Denny Trent, the school's principal, appearing at his door for their final chat. Inwardly, Jon dreaded the conversation.

The soft knock and the reluctant voice that came from behind the half-closed door surprised him. "Mr. Shepherd?"

It was Holly Pembroke, a student from his seventh grade history class. She brought a warm smile to his face. She hadn't taken part in the flurry of remarks tossed his direction as the other seventh graders had filed out. Even now she looked hesitant to speak, but throughout the year they had seemed to understand each other and Jon was quite sure he knew what she would say.

"I didn't mean to bother you, it's just . . . well, I wanted to thank you. You taught me so much—about history being important and all. The things you said—it just made history seem almost *real*, and I never thought about it that way before." She paused, as if to gather courage. "I don't know who they'll get to replace you, but there's just nobody who can teach like you."

"Thanks, Holly." Jon smiled, looking down at her slight frame and almost feeling shy himself, knowing how much the conversation meant to Holly.

There was more she wanted to say. Her dark eyes did not rise to meet his and her hands fidgeted with her backpack, but she clearly intended to speak her mind before she allowed herself to retreat into the hallway.

"I don't understand why they're making you leave. And I don't think they're right. I mean, it's not like you didn't teach what was in the textbooks or anything. Jennie said you just told the class that you didn't really agree. I mean, we're supposed to be learning about all kinds of ideas—that's what they all keep telling us—and they don't even let you be honest about what *you* believe." Holly was getting worked up now; the tears were beginning to form. Selfishly, Jon needed to listen—to be told he was wonderful and that he had done nothing wrong—but he knew that was not in Holly's best interest.

"Do you remember when we studied about 'due process,' Holly?" He coaxed her to listen, ducking his head to try to draw her eyes up to his.

"Yes," she sniffed, nervously pushing long brown strands behind her ears.

"That's all this is. It's due process. I can't be considered guilty until *after* my hearing, and that's probably a few weeks away. Hopefully I can make people understand what really happened. But it is *fair* for them to ask for a hearing. There were students who didn't think I had a right to say what I did in a public school science classroom. There were parents who agreed. These people do have a right to question what I teach. It's okay."

"But they're making you look like a criminal! They're talking like you weren't a good teacher—and you are. Everybody knows you are. And, besides, you were only teaching Mrs. Jennings' science class for a couple days. Why can't they just let you keep teaching history? Science isn't even your class."

"That gets complicated, Holly—and wouldn't satisfy the people who are asking for this inquiry. But it's not over, right? It's really just started. And I'll have a chance to defend myself. Hey," he smiled with a wink, "it's history in action."

She had peeked up long enough to smile back.

"It's okay, Holly. Don't worry. Just be glad you won't have to take that Civil War exam I was working on. It was gonna be a killer."

Holly laughed then, relieved that he had given her permission, relieved that she could see him smiling, too.

"Hey, how's your little brother doing?"

"He's okay. His ankle wasn't even really broken. It just swelled a lot."

"That's good."

"I guess I'll see ya?"

"Yeah, I'll be around."

With a nod and a smile, Holly retreated into the hall. Jon could only sigh deeply. This was hard . . . really hard. The words *"they're making you look like a criminal"* kept echoing in his mind. Is that what he looked like—a criminal—for speaking what he believed was truth?

Almost immediately, Denny appeared at the door, as expected. After speaking with Holly, Jon hoped this conversation would be less emotionally wrenching.

"Need some help with those boxes, Jon?"

"Sure."

Each man hoisted a box and headed for the employee parking area. Conversation did not come easily. It was Jon who broke the silence. "Have you found a substitute teacher for my classes yet?"

"Well, Murray Surrell will sub for Government, and we've got LaNae Beal again for German. And it looks like we're going to use Eddie Blake for American History and World Civ."

Jon frowned. "I thought you'd be looking for another substitute. Eddie's on staff, and he's already got three classes. How long are you thinking this is going to take, Denny?"

"We told Eddie these are just temporary classes for him. Actually, that's the only reason we could get him to agree. He's got a great mind for numbers, but he sure hates the idea of teaching history."

Jon frowned again. "Well, that doesn't make me feel any better. Now my history classes are being turned over to a guy who can't stand to teach them. You might as well count these next weeks as a washout. Couldn't Walter Kreuger come back to teach for the interim?"

"That gets tricky now that he's officially retired."

Jon could feel his frustration growing. He forced himself to speak cautiously. "I know you're doing the best you can, Denny, but I can't help thinking it's the kids who are going to suffer in the end. Eddie can't teach history any more effectively than I could teach math, but that doesn't change the fact that this whole class of kids is going to miss foundational information. I hate to sound dramatic, Denny, but—think about it—we're studying the Civil War now. They are going to hear three more weeks of Civil War from Eddie Blake. Would you want him teaching history to your own kids?"

"No. No, you're right. And if you have a better idea I'd be glad to hear it. But he'll have your plan book. That'll help."

A familiar sense of guilt fell over Jon. "I tend to improvise a lot, Denny. Remember? It took me so long to try to get my plans to you that we agreed you'd let me get by with using the curriculum outline if I actually taught most of what was there—but in my own style. That outline is going to be dry as bones in Eddie's hands. He's not going to enhance it at all." Jon's mind was racing now. "Hey, I could jot down some of my ideas. Maybe get him to talk with Ruth in Home Ec to work up the costumes the kids were planning. She'd help him. She offered before."

"Jon," Denny cut in, "Eddie won't be doing costumes. It's not going to happen."

"But the kids are so much more willing to learn if they have some kind of project they can really get interested in. Isn't there any way you can—"

"Look, I've been over this again and again. It just keeps coming back to what I *can* do, not what I *want*. I *want* this to just disappear—to never have happened at all."

Jon popped the hatch on his car and set the boxes inside. "And I wish *that* as much as anyone." He slammed the hatch and faced Denny squarely, sucking in the cool February air.

"You know I didn't mean for this to happen. You understand that, right?"

"I know you weren't looking for a fight, Jon." Then he laughed dryly. "But I'll bet if you had it to do over again, you wouldn't change a thing, would you? You know, it's kind of my fault. If I would have just kept you teaching history, like you were supposed to—like your contract said—this wouldn't have happened. But, no, I had to push my luck. I had to take a good history teacher and put him in a science class. How does a guy who's used to kicking around ideas and interpretations in history teach science? . . . Well, you started discussing and *wham!* you got yourself suspended."

Jon couldn't share the humor Denny was trying to inject into the situation. "Thanks for the help, Denny."

Darkness had already fallen by the time Jon pulled into the driveway of his rented home. Utterly exhausted from the day, he needed a chance to kick off his shoes, put his feet up, and pet his dog for a while with a good CD playing. But most of all, he knew he needed to spend some time praying.

❧ ❧ ❧ ❧

Two meager swaths of light struggled to find a way for the car between the winding rows of palmetto trees. They gave only vague clues to the twisted, narrow track of asphalt. Esther felt her own eyes searching, too, groping for some sign of what might lay hidden beyond the headlight beams. It was amazing that the highway and suburban Atlanta shopping areas they had just passed could dissolve so quickly into this tangle of trees and narrow road.

"Are you sure you didn't take a wrong turn, Neal?" Her voice cut the cool night air.

"Now, sugar," he laughed back, "don't you think I know where I'm going? You just sit back and close your eyes. We're close now." With a wide grin, Neal chuckled delightedly.

Esther forced her eyes closed. She hated surprises—had always hated the feeling of being maneuvered by someone else—had hated knowing that she would be required to perform the overwhelming task of being elated by whatever lay ahead of her, even though she was most often disappointed.

A sudden lurch of the car brought them to a stop.

"Keep 'em closed," Neal prodded. She could hear the click of his door being opened and then the thud as it shut again. His footsteps were slow and deliberate as he passed in front of the car, a sure sign that he was taking time to enjoy his own anticipation. Then chilling night air swept against her legs as he pulled open her door.

"Here's my hand, darlin'."

Esther took it, swinging her new leather pumps out onto the ground beside the car and cringing at the thought that she wouldn't see any mud until it was too late. Cautiously, she stepped along beside Neal, clutching the sleeve of his suit coat with both hands.

"Step up," he instructed. Esther could almost feel his broad smile pulling tight laugh lines across his face. "That was just one step; now we've got four more up ahead. Okay, sugar, here's the next one."

They were on a wooden porch now; she could hear the hollow echo of their footsteps beneath her. Surely, surely, Neal would not bring her to a dinner party without giving her fair warning. Whose home could this be?

"Open wide," he whispered against her hair.

They *were* on a porch, a broad one that ran the full length of a very large brick house. Georgian columns and a row of curving white spindles swept along its front edge, holding back the shadows of bushes and lawn. Two full-length etched-glass windows spilled soft, warm light around the rich green of the front door, crowned by a stained-glass panel above. On either side, a pair of perfectly symmetrical windows guarded the front, offering no indication of what lay behind. It was a splendid entry to what must be an astonishing home.

"Who lives here?" Esther gasped, barely suppressing her growing interest.

"Well, let's just see who's home."

"Neal," she whispered fiercely, "tell me."

Without pausing to knock, Neal punched four numbers into the security panel and then grasped the brass knob. The door swung open. Esther could feel herself grow rigid, not comprehending what was happening.

There was not a sound from inside the house. The only light came from a doorway on the far side of the oversized entry. Esther could feel Neal's hand on her back, guiding her in, but her mind refused to make any sense of the moment. Then Neal reached around Esther for the light switch, one hand still under her arm, keeping her close to him.

Instantly light filled the room. A large and graceful staircase with glossy, polished cherry railings appeared in front of Esther. The entryway floor was also wood, a variety of kinds and stains, intricately laid out to produce a striking octagonal pattern. Her eyes traveled in a moment from one splendid corner of the vaulted room to the next. To her left was a shadowed doorway into a room that seemed empty. Ahead was what appeared to be a hallway tucking itself back under the stair landing.

She turned her face up to Neal's, her mind still failing to understand.

"It's yours." Neal's voice was husky with feeling. "It's ours."

Esther could feel her heart squeeze inside her chest. Slowly, her eyes swept the room again, trying to absorb the incomprehensible.

"It's what you said you wanted, isn't it?"

She could only nod dumbly.

"I knew it the first time I laid eyes on it. It just felt like you, darlin'."

He came to life then. With one hand clutching hers, Neal pulled Esther through the house, touring first one room and then another. His words were breathless with excitement as he pointed out each of the home's attributes. The living room with a ten-foot coffered ceiling and carved oak fireplace mantel. The shimmering chandelier in the large dining room, reflecting off French doors that led to a covered porch. The huge, vaulted kitchen opening onto a cozy breakfast nook with bay window, and a family room whose stone fireplace massed against one full wall. Esther was dazed by the beauty she saw and her mind refused to think beyond the view before her.

Finally he stopped and searched her eyes. "You *do* like it, don't you?"

"I . . . I don't know what to say, Neal." Esther's words were too loud for the enormous empty spaces around her. She could feel her eyes drop, her mind still clouded and refusing to be useful. The silence was long and heavy. "I *want* to be excited with you. It's just so sudden."

"You don't take well to surprises, do you, darlin'? I think I understand." Neal's words came easier then; his tension seemed to seep away, though his gaze was still intense. Esther dropped her cheek against his shoulder, not certain whose heart was pounding harder, his or her own.

At last she struggled to speak. "This doesn't change anything. You understand that, don't you? We've talked about this, Neal. We can't live together until after we're married. I know it's still a few months away, but I really want to wait." Esther could not bring herself to look up.

There was no response to her question. Conversation seemed to have become impossible as both grappled with their own thoughts.

"Let's go" was his only answer.

# Three

*Friday, February 19*

Morning was welcome when it finally came. Esther had spent a great deal of the night pacing the floor and trying to sort out her feelings. It was comforting to begin the familiar routine. Making orange juice, showering, dressing for work; all this she could do in the stillness of her apartment without having to think. When the ringing of her telephone shattered the silence, Esther was relieved to discover that it was work related.

"If I were you, I'd wear your navy suit with that really cute vest. Robin will be in today. It's already time for this month's meeting with management, and the buzz around here is that big things will happen. You'd better be ready for anything." Annie herself was always a step or two ahead.

"What are people saying?" Esther questioned, already slipping off her shoes and heading back into her bedroom to change clothes, tucking the cordless phone between her shoulder and cheek.

"Nobody's saying what it is; they're just sure something's up. You know Watt—he's always trying to make a big impression on Robin, and he knows this will be his only crack at it this month. I'll bet you my next raise they're deciding on another news anchor now that it looks like Sybil Horn is out."

"What?" Esther hadn't heard this latest update. "They fired her? I knew she'd get a reprimand, but I never dreamed they'd fire her."

"They haven't officially let her go yet. But that's sure to be the main topic in their meeting today."

"I agree she made a poor choice in refusing to read Watt's story on air, but—fire her? That seems pretty harsh to me." Esther rehung her beige skirt and grabbed her blue suit off its hanger.

"You just don't do your own thing in the news game. You have to play by the rules, and Watt is clearly in charge of who says what around here. The way I see it, they've *got* to fire her. How could they do any less? She caused havoc. Just think about it. When Sybil launched into her own agenda on air, everybody was affected—the cameramen, the TelePrompTer operator, the control room. The floor manager must have gone crazy! They didn't know how long she'd go on or where in the script she'd be willing to pick up again or anything. It was a mess—a terrible breach of protocol."

"I guess." Esther hesitated. "But shouldn't Watt take some of the blame?"

"Who's going to be the one to point his direction? Robin is the only one who could do that, and the only time he meets with any of us, Watt's around. Who's going to have the nerve to stand up in front of Robin and, with Watt sitting right there, criticize what happens on that set? No way, Esther. It's not going to happen. Nobody's that brave—or that stupid."

"So they expect the anchors to stop thinking and just read the script?"

"They get their shot in the editorial meeting; after that they have to play it the way it falls."

"Hmm. Who do you think they'll put in her place?" Esther frowned at her reflection in her bedroom mirror, wondering if she should put her shoulder-length hair up in a chignon.

"Well, now that this happened, Watt's sure to want a 'yes' person in her place. Anyway, they will probably be interviewing quickly and quietly for this. Now, don't jump to conclusions, but I heard that your name came up a couple of times. I'm not sure how you fit into all this. You don't really have enough years of experience as a reporter at a station this size to be in the running for anchor, but I have a feeling that our newsroom is in for some restructuring. It's no day to fade into the furniture. Just show up looking good and smiling big. That's all I'm saying."

Esther was always amazed at how much information Annie was able to glean while working in the tape room. It was hard to believe she didn't secretly run the place, but that was Annie. Ever since they had shared a dorm room in college, she had been able to find the pulse of the action, regardless of the obstacles.

"When does Robin get to the station?"

"About two o'clock. He's scheduled a meeting for one-thirty here, but he's taking Watt and the other program managers to lunch first. They'll probably take a *long* lunch and end up pulling in around two."

"I'm already wearing the blue suit. So I'll be on my way in just a few minutes. Put the coffee on, Annie. I'll be living on it this morning."

"Late night with the honey man?"

"Annie! No, Neal and I . . . oh, forget it. I'll tell you when I get there."

For a few moments, during the conversation about work, Esther had been able to lay aside her turbulent thoughts about Neal and the new house. Now that Annie had reminded her again, Esther caught herself chewing a fingernail while waiting for the traffic light to change on her way to the station. Annoyed with herself, she clutched the wheel firmly with both hands, searching around for a distraction.

Her eyes darted from storefronts to billboards. Then for

a brief moment she exchanged eye contact with a man in the passenger seat of the car next to hers. In a fraction of a second, she noticed his absentminded expression flicker with interest at spying her. His face lit with a smile of delight, very familiar to Esther, and he even offered her a little wave in recognition. Esther smiled politely in return, then brought her eyes back to the road in front of her, deliberately avoiding any further chance for communication with him.

This display of interest occurred so often that Esther hardly noticed anymore. She had first received the revelation that her looks brought special attention after winning a fourth grade spelling bee. At first, it had seemed strange to her that her best friend, Andy Gray, the winner of the boys' competition, had been congratulated by the well-wishers for his performance, while comments directed at her seemed to be about how nice she looked, how very pretty—and how poised. Gradually, she had come to understand that she was indeed different in this way—at least to people who had not taken the time to really know her. Andy and her close friends, however, had never treated her any differently.

There had been a period in her teen years when she had liked the attention, had even sought it out. Then her attitude changed and she had grown annoyed by it—tired of being surveyed by nameless and often tactless men, usually much older than herself, who acknowledged her looks and not her accomplishments. Finally, just as she entered college, Esther resolved that her beauty was simply a fact and that the less she considered it the better off she'd be.

With Esther's no-nonsense approach to adult life, vanity had not really been a temptation. She had not chosen long legs, elegant facial features, and flowing blond hair any more than Annie had chosen to be a petite, pixie-nosed, fiery redhead. She was also modest enough to know the difference between the narrow constraints of "commercially accepted" beauty and the less definable attributes of what she considered to be true beauty—eyes that held warmth and honesty, a demeanor that was friendly and personable.

Take Neal, for instance. It was true his complexion was ruddy and pocked, but he was also quick to smile and had what Esther considered to be adorable laugh lines. Never had he failed to offer her encouragement and sympathy. Never had he chosen to ignore her needs. Of course, it was true he was a little short-tempered with Annie, but then, Annie provoked him, too. Overall, Esther considered Neal to be a very attractive man—confident, impeccably dressed, and unique in his particular style of colorfully southern graciousness. That was the kind of beauty she considered to be real.

However, where business was concerned, she admitted she felt very differently. If it was a professional advantage to be attractive, why should she consider it wrong to use her looks favorably? She hadn't asked to be set apart in this way. Beauty was simply an attribute to be managed and applied, and Esther had chosen and pursued a career carefully—with *all* things considered.

Of course, involvement in news media was also in her family background. That had helped her make the decision. Her grandfather had worked in the newspaper business for years. His reputation was known far beyond their small Nebraska town where he had maintained his private home. Her grandmother had often fussed about how often he was required to travel, but he had managed to earn several prestigious awards for his work. He had been the one who had encouraged Esther to go into television. In fact, he had really given her the courage to try.

As Esther entered the downtown Atlanta station, she could not help noticing the definite air of excitement hanging over the building. Esther swiped her badge through the security scanner, eyeing the personnel at the reception area suspiciously. Yes, something *was* up, and Esther was not sure she liked the feeling. Stepping through the heavy security door, she determined to keep an eye on the goings-on around her.

The early-morning news was aired and the editorial meeting came and went with no hint of a bomb being dropped. The decision had been made to use a piece for tomorrow's show that Esther had completed last week, leaving her with a relatively free morning—which in the news business simply meant there was no pressing story to chase. Instead, there was only the mountain of things that were supposed to have been accomplished but had been postponed during all the previous emergencies. That fact gave an ominous feel to a day behind her desk.

As she passed Annie's door on her way back, she gestured that nothing noteworthy had transpired in the meeting. Annie shrugged but nodded her approval at Esther's attire.

*How ludicrous*, Esther thought. *I'm twenty-nine and still getting caught up in rumors like a schoolgirl.*

For some time, Esther worked at the desk in her cubicle, returning telephone calls, scheduling appointments, writing memos—and shutting out the hum around her. This was the part of her job that she liked least; it was far more interesting to be pursuing stories and discussing news than playing phone tag with business associates. Finally, she leaned back in her chair, stretching her arms above her head. The blouse she had chosen was too tight around her neck, and Esther was annoyed that she had made her decision to wear it based on Annie's premonition.

Reaching for her coffee cup and finding it empty, Esther decided to stretch her legs. Maybe she would even stop by the tape room to see if Annie was there. It wasn't likely, since she seemed to be masterful at finding excuses to roam, but there was always a chance, and Esther had a word or two for her friend.

Winding through the short maze of desks and co-workers in the newsroom, Esther turned a corner and found herself face-to-face with Watt Shreve, the news director for the station and, even more alarmingly, Robin Kincaid, who virtually owned the entire operation. It was only twelve-thirty.

"Excuse me," she fumbled, forcing herself to recover her composure.

"I should say," Watt snapped back. All five feet nine inches of Watt Shreve's thin frame seemed cocked like a mousetrap, always ready to snap whoever was unfortunate enough to be closest to him—especially when Robin was present.

But it was Robin who took command. Without blinking, his blue eyes, intense and thorough, measured Esther from head to toe, seeming to read her thoughts as well. "Have we been introduced?" His question was deeply thoughtful.

"My name is Esther Branson, Mr. Kincaid." Now that her breath had returned, Esther could feel confidence sweeping over her. Not about to let the opportunity slip away, she continued in a charming tone. "I've worked with the station for three years, but I'm afraid I've not had the pleasure of being introduced to you." Her smile was perfect; she could feel it. Her back was straight, her eyes glowing.

"That *is* unfortunate. I'm glad we were able to resolve that problem, Miss Branson." Esther was surprised to find that Robin was very much a gentleman—even handsome, with graying hair lying perfectly in place and age adding softness to the features of his intense face. He was not at all what Esther had envisioned.

Watt was just beginning to catch up. "Esther is responsible for the piece we aired in January about the new orphanages." He withheld comment, waiting for a clue from Robin, ready to go either way.

"I'm familiar with her work. I make it a point to be acquainted with everyone's work." He gave the rebuke without even glancing toward Watt. Then his eyes glimmered with a smile. "That was a good piece."

"Yes, we all thought so." Watt was still trying to regain Robin's attention.

"Well, Miss Branson." Robin's eyes were locked on her own, as if still assessing her. "I've a feeling we'll meet again . . . soon."

"I look forward to it." Esther returned his parting smile, withdrew her hand, and, being careful to appear relaxed, continued down the hallway.

It was some time before Esther could breathe again. A quick step into the copier room gave her a moment to slow her heartbeat. Her mind replayed the meeting. Watt's taut expression, Robin's aloof casualness, her own jump-started confidence.

Robin had been wonderful—Watt had been disgusting. Esther loathed the way he paraded himself when Robin was around, begging to be noticed. Then Esther looked down at her own blue suit and vest, and an awful thought descended over her. *How was my own behavior any different?* The question brought a twinge of guilt.

It *was* different. She couldn't really put it into words, but she was certain that her own ambition was not at all the same as Watt's. In fact, it was ridiculous to compare the two. And so, Esther forced the difficult question from her mind for the time being. She would find Annie instead.

❧ ❧ ❧ ❧

Jon was restless. At first he had tried to convince himself that there was enough work at home to keep himself busy, but even the first morning away from his job was not going particularly well. The possibility of weeks of waiting ahead of him was more than he could stand. Finally, he gave up creating activity in the small house he shared with his brother and headed out in his car for the youth center where they each worked part time.

The starting of the youth center was what had brought Jon and Caleb to Atlanta from Wisconsin four years earlier. Jon had transferred to a new school system. Caleb had come south with Jon to work at the center while finishing college, eventually earning a master's degree in business.

For Jon it had been an obvious calling, but it was far more complex for Caleb. With a mind for management, he didn't share Jon's passion for youth work. Sometimes, in the beginning, Jon wondered if Caleb really believed that the center would succeed.

Added to this was the unspoken fact that they did not even truly share a family tie. Jon was really an only child. Seven-year-old Caleb and his own younger brother had been adopted by the Shepherd family when Jon was in his mid-teens. The three boys had spent a couple of short years living together, had even enjoyed one another's company, but hadn't really had a chance to feel like "brothers" before Jon had packed up for college.

In the back of his mind, he wondered why Caleb had chosen to follow him south, but he was grateful. Over and over again, Jon had learned to appreciate Caleb in new ways. In fact, everyone at the center had come to depend on Caleb, too. While Caleb had less vision than Jon, he was certainly much more organized and practical. The staff probably could not have succeeded in drawing together the various inner-city churches for the interdenominational youth center without Caleb and his ability to mediate—nor without his tenacity for working through the myriad of details in obtaining, financing, and equipping the building itself.

It was a forty-five-minute drive to the youth center. Leaning back in the driver's seat, Jon flipped on the radio and settled into the line of traffic heading into the heart of the city. Music rose and fell around him, drivers traded lanes in a perpetual dance, but Jon felt alone—isolated among the thousands who were swarming nearby, all oblivious to the fact that his world had ground to a halt.

The lesson. What had it been about, anyway? That last-minute "can you fill in?" lesson in science class. The layers of earth? Yes, the students had all brought him up to speed on their last studies—or at least as much as junior high students were willing to share. Perhaps they had just chosen a recent topic that interested them most. At any rate, they had described to him the age of the layers of earth strata—and gave a vague attempt to explain an upcoming project. They were supposed to go outside to gather soil samples. *Sure* they were! He could review the textbook topic if nothing else, but there was no way he was being duped into taking them all outdoors.

So what question was it that had sparked so much discussion? Oh yes, he had asked why all the earth's layers were laid out in such parallel lines if they had each formed individually. Sure, he had acknowledged, there were lots of places where the layers of crust seemed to have shifted, folded, or broken—but still, the layers themselves all seemed to have lain evenly before that. If they were each so very old and had formed so many thousands of years apart, where were the signs of erosion and ancient rivers, windswept earth dunes and earthquake disturbances in each of the separate layers? Why hadn't some layers settled at odd angles? Why did they all seem to be so perfectly parallel?

A red car zipped into the space in front of Jon, inches away from his bumper. With quick reflexes, he tapped the brakes and his thoughts were snapped back to the present. "Would it kill you to signal?" he muttered at the unseen driver. Running a hand through the wave of brown hair that hung against his forehead, he checked over his right shoulder, signaled, and pulled aside to fill up with gas. He didn't really need it just now, but maybe a soda would clear his head.

Back on the street and nearing the youth center, his thoughts returned to the infamous classroom discussion.

*"Mr. Shepherd, if the earth's layers were all formed at the same time, how did they form?"*

*"Interesting question. Anybody have an idea? Anybody here been to a creation science seminar? Nobody?"*

Well, he'd been to one. That was quite a while ago, but he could still recall some of the basic ideas.

The speaker at the seminar had suggested that the Great Flood of the Bible had caused the layers. Even now, Jon could feel himself smile at the students' reaction. They were always more than willing to laugh at new ideas. Wise cracks had followed. These remarks had never bothered Jon. He believed that if you were too insecure to take a few pointed comments here and there, you'd better not choose to teach young teens. No, he hadn't minded at all. He had even laughed a little with them. But he hadn't backed down either. *"Doesn't anyone remember their studies about ancient cultures from last year?"* So many ancient civilizations from all around the world had lore about a great flood and a family that had survived it. Was it reasonable to believe that the peoples from each of the continents had made up the same type of legend?

Sure, it was possible they had heard the stories when explorers had come, but then, why was each flood story unique to each culture? Why did the Incas say the llamas and their keepers went up on a tall mountain, while Jewish Scriptures spoke of a large boat? Wouldn't missionaries to the Incas have mentioned the boat? So why wouldn't those stories be the same?

And if there had been a great worldwide flood, couldn't it have eroded massive amounts of earth, then allowed the soils to settle out in layers? Hadn't each of the students done that experiment in elementary school—shaken water and earth together and watched it settle into layers—perfectly parallel layers?

*"What if . . ."* Jon had asked them.

*"How can you seriously think that?"* they had questioned back.

*"I don't know if I do, but what if . . ."* he had persisted. Funny, there hadn't seemed to be much more to that day's discussion.

That night, Jon had done some research. He had rummaged through the local Christian bookstore for books about creation science, purchasing all four that he had found. Late into the night, he had read page after page. By morning, he had been ready to discuss further. By morning, he had unwittingly laid out his own path to trouble.

His intentions had been good. When he scooped up the two most useful books on the topic of creation and the defense of a young earth, he had fully intended to have them approved by Denny and to double-check the idea of presenting the information to the students. But halfway through their conversation Denny had been called back to the office. His offhanded "Do what you want to, I'm sure it's fine" comment seemed reasonable to both of them at the time. Neither would have guessed where the discussion of the day would take them.

*"Here, let me introduce you to the Hydroplate Theory,"* Jon had begun. Just a theory, he had been careful to state. Hadn't they heard him? Was the girl who later ranted to her mother about that "religious fanatic teacher" checking her makeup or writing a note to a friend when he had explained the concept of "theory"? Was that atheist boy who rallied the other students against him privately calculating the money he'd saved for college while the others discussed facts versus opinions? At any rate, between the time afternoon classes had ended and the bell rang the next morning, there had surfaced a sufficient quantity of calls and notes addressed to Jon, Denny, and the school board to warrant an official investigation. Jon had been called out of fourth-period history class and asked to use the remaining part of that day to gather his

belongings for a short, "friendly" break from the classroom—for the "peace of mind of all involved."

Amazing how quickly one's world could begin spinning in an opposite direction. . . .

At last, Jon's Honda bounced over the low curb and into the makeshift parking lot of the youth center. The ritual of unlocking the ten-foot gate, driving through, and re-locking it followed. It always made Jon feel as if he were lowering and raising a drawbridge to a medieval fortress, but a glance at the refuse scattered around and the graffiti scrawled on the buildings reminded him of the realities of inner-city life. Maybe these kids did need a castle to protect them, after all.

The heavy metal door slammed behind him as he walked into the center. "Hello," he called to the stillness. "Anybody here?"

No answer.

Wandering into the makeshift gym, Jon slipped out of his school jacket, letting it drop on the first row of folding chairs. He picked up a stray basketball lying deserted along a wall. Just a few minutes of shooting, then he'd find some work to do.

# Four

*Friday, February 19*

It had been in the back of Esther's mind that she would try to stumble across Robin again sometime later in the day. That proved to be wishful thinking. Shortly after meeting him for the first time, she received a page from the tip line that a new telephone scam had been discovered in the local area. Esther hurried to gather more information, hoping to have enough to include in her next evening segment.

For two hours she made phone calls, getting closer and closer to the story, unraveling detail after detail. By the time Esther had gathered enough information to write up a rough draft of the story and turn it in, she was certain that Robin was long gone. In just half an hour she was due in makeup and then her segment would be taped for the evening news. Pushing herself back from her computer while the printer droned nearby, she eagerly anticipated the approaching end to her workday.

Esther expected to arrive home in time to flip on her own television set and watch the station's evening news while she popped a low-cal frozen dinner into the microwave. And by the time the last segment aired she would have her feet up on the coffee table and an empty TV dinner tray rinsed and tucked away in her recycling bin. *Quite a life! Exciting? Per-*

*haps not.* But Esther liked the structure and comfort that she had discovered along the way, and she still hoped to progress further in her career once she had gained more experience.

Her printing done and her mind now back on work, she thumbed through her pink copy of the newscast script to check for changes in the story she had previously turned in and was pleased to see that only minor edits had been made.

"Esther." Annie's strained voice interrupted her thoughts.

"What is it?"

Annie peered into the neighboring cubicle, then confided nervously, "Robin is still here. He's in the last conference room—the small one by the back entrance. And Watt is flying around the office making phone calls and looking panicky. I just heard him tell Mark to call you in." Her eyes locked on Esther's.

"Why?"

"I don't know." For Annie this was a bewildering admission. "I don't have a clue."

"I guess I'll just go talk to him." Esther's stomach had knotted. "I hope it's not bad news."

"Good luck" was all that Annie could offer, weakly.

Forcing her fears to the back of her mind, Esther walked directly to Watt's office, not even allowing herself a deep breath before knocking on the oak door.

"Who is it?" came the muffled response.

She pushed the door open enough to peek around it and answered, "I was told you were looking for me."

"Yes, Branson. Come in."

Watt gathered himself up from behind his desk and walked to the file cabinet. From it he withdrew a stack of papers as Esther dropped stiffly into a side chair. "You're aware, of course, that I met with Mr. Kincaid today." Esther nodded.

"During our meeting, an issue with one of our evening

news anchors was voiced and resolved. Sybil Horn will no longer be with our news team."

Esther could only hope that the flood of thoughts and questions coming to her mind were not displayed on her face. Watt continued, "We will, consequently, be needing to find a replacement for her. Jared O'Neal seemed the obvious choice, but, as I pointed out in the meeting, we cannot become the only local station without a female co-anchor. And there were other issues to be considered." Watt's expression and his voice were tense. "We have other reporters with more experience and, frankly, better presentation than you, but I have asked Robin to consider you."

Esther was shocked and somewhat apprehensive. The fleeting, awful thought occurred to her that if she were to be offered the co-anchor position, she would be coming face-to-face with Watt on a much more regular basis.

"The bottom line, Branson, is you made it onto the list of applicants. And since we don't have any time before tonight's broadcast, Mr. Kincaid is waiting in Conference Room D to interview you for the temporary, and possibly permanent, position. You'll need to go there now."

What could she say? In stunned silence, Esther rose to obey.

"I've taken a risk in suggesting you, Branson. Don't blow it."

Esther's mind was still reeling, but her legs carried her down the hall to where she rapped on the last door, forcing herself to do so with a firm hand. Her heart was not feeling the confidence that her knock projected. Once again, she opened the door upon hearing the response from inside.

"Miss Branson, please come in."

"Good afternoon, Mr. Kincaid."

"Please, sit down." Esther took her seat along the near side of the conference table, looking across at him in fear. The bright sunshine coming through the window behind Robin framed him in a luminescent haze, giving the effect of a royal appearance. The wide oak chair became a throne and the full-length coat that he had draped across the back of it, a robe. Esther glanced down at her lap in an effort to recover her sensibilities.

"Shreve has briefed you on our dilemma?"

"Yes, sir. I understand it."

"Then let me be as efficient as possible. What do you believe qualifies you to fill this position?" His eyes were piercing hers, waiting for an answer, and Esther knew that this moment would determine much of what would happen in her future career, whether she was prepared for it or not. But Neal had already asked her similar questions, had grilled her to be ready so that she wouldn't be forced to think on her feet. Instantly, the words came back to her.

"I have made TV news both my occupation and my life-style, Mr. Kincaid. I do have a resumé on file with this station, which will give my educational background, and I have no doubt that you are aware of those qualifications. I have also striven personally to be well educated. It is my goal to be a reporter with breadth and depth of knowledge.

"For instance, as a consumer reporter, I didn't allow myself to just go after the story. I made sure that I understood all aspects of it—the financial implications, the unspoken codes of the business world, and the reactions from each group of people involved. I'm certain that this is the reason I've been well received by the public and also by the sponsors. I've been referred to as 'thorough' and 'fair-minded,' because I make it my responsibility to know my stories inside and out."

For a moment, Esther faltered. Robin was not looking up—and he wasn't writing notes. He seemed to be thinking. Esther wasn't sure whether to go on or to wait for his attention. She decided to continue.

"In addition to my own story assignments, I have made

it a point to be very well-read on other topics. I subscribe to several national and international magazines, which I read cover to cover. I am a regular at my local public library and on the Internet, where I sample a broad range of topics and stay abreast of the newest publications."

"And your experience?" Robin broke in dutifully. "What do you have to say about your having less experience than usual for this position?"

There was something encouraging in his tone that, though his words sounded short, made Esther sure he was being won over. She charged ahead. "I have enough experience for you to know that I *can* perform well on camera. I also have enough exposure that you can be sure the public accepts me—and trusts me. However, I am still a fresh face to them, and I don't carry with me any negative history. No one will be saying, 'Esther Branson—sure, she used to be on channel X, and she really blew it during the hostage affair,' or 'I liked her a lot better when she used to do thus and so,' or 'when she used to wear her hair another way.' " Esther was eyeing Robin carefully, noting his expression, his posture, and the way he had moved forward in his chair.

She paused, waiting while he considered her words. The last thing she wanted to do was say one word beyond what was working in her favor.

Robin was still looking down at the paper work in front of him. "I believe I have all the information I need. I do have your resumé from the station's files, and I've already requested a sample of your recent work from the tape room."

Esther smiled, knowing that Annie would be the one preparing the "sample."

"You'll need to be available in about an hour. We'll let you know when our final decision is made." Then he looked up, as if as an afterthought. "Do you have any questions?"

"No, I don't at this time, Mr. Kincaid."

"Fine. Then, if you'll excuse me."

Esther rose and walked back out of the room, for the first time conscious that she was trembling. Had it really gone well, or was that just misinterpretation on her part? Robin had hardly even looked at her, but somehow he seemed pleased just the same.

For about an hour, Esther paced back and forth, hiding in the copier room, feigning an attempt to put the questions out of her mind by making a number of photocopies for documentation that she had been neglecting for some time. However, she realized there was no way to calm her nerves just now.

And then she started at the sound of her pager buzzing. The message that she should come to Watt's office scrolled across the display.

"We've made our decision." Watt was getting straight to the point. "You'll be our new co-anchor. You'll start tonight. Do you have any questions?" Again she was being asked if she had questions.

Questions? Of course she had questions. "That will be fine. Thank you," she heard her own voice answer. "When can I pick up my copy of the script for tonight?"

Watt seemed surprised at her composure—but then, Esther was surprised herself.

He turned toward his desk as a way of dismissing her, tossing over his shoulder, "Pick up the blue copy in the printer room now and be out of makeup by five. Oh, and there'll be a new contract on your desk tomorrow for you to sign. And, of course, that would be your new desk in Horn's old office."

That was it. As she marched back up the hallway that only moments before she had walked down, she couldn't believe how quickly it had taken place. How did she feel? She wasn't sure. There were so many thoughts to be sorted through. But most of all, she kept hearing Watt's earlier words, "other reporters with more experience and, frankly, better presentation," and "other issues to be considered." Why had Watt recommended her? Why had he been in favor of promoting her when he had never seemed to show her the least bit of interest before? Maybe the mere fact that she was a woman had tipped the scales in her favor. But, nonetheless, Esther was still wary. She'd have to prove to Watt that she was capable—whatever his reasons for supporting her.

❧ ❧ ❧ ❧

Jon had only been at the youth center for about an hour before he had begun working. He knew it had been agreed upon that the boys' locker room needed painting, so he decided now was as good a time as any. For two hours he rolled paint back and forth, changing yellowed walls to blue—stretching and straining to make his way around exposed plumbing and shower stalls. He painted everything—lockers, metal benches, and heating vents. The work was satisfying—requiring no thought. It was just what he needed.

At about four o'clock he stepped back to survey his work. It was blue. He'd say that much. Anyway, it looked clean and fresh. That was enough.

Unfortunately, it would be an hour or two before anyone else was due to arrive. That still left him with time to spare. With brush and paint tray piled in a sink and soaking, Jon wandered to the offices and then into one of the classrooms. Dropping into a chair in the corner, Jon pulled a book out of his coat pocket and flipped to the marked page. He hadn't had a chance to finish reading this science book yet. There were questions that he still wanted answered. Not for the students now, but for himself. In moments, he was lost in its pages. Reading like a teacher, he grabbed a pen from the table beside him and scribbled notes to himself in a pocket-sized notebook with tattered edges.

By five-thirty, the sound of doors closing and people

moving began to be heard around Jon, but he didn't notice. Footsteps came and went in the hallway, but his attentions were elsewhere, completely engrossed in his reading. At last, he was pulled back to reality by a hand shaking his shoulder. "Jon . . . man, are you in there?"

"Hey, Caleb. When did you get here?"

"Oh, about half an hour ago. We've been laughing at you in the office. You must really be concentrating. I guess you didn't hear any of us come in. What're you reading?"

"Some books about creation science. It's interesting."

"I guess so. Hey, are you planning to coach tonight or what?"

Jon shut the book and stretched. "Yeah, I am. Is it after five? I haven't had anything to eat yet."

"I thought you might be hungry, so I bought a bucket of chicken on my way in. But you'd better hurry. There were still a few pieces when I left it in the office, but I can't promise they'll be there for long. By the way, Mom called to see if you're okay. I wasn't sure what to tell her. Are you okay?"

"Yeah. I guess I am. Just bored out of my mind."

"Well, you can tell her *that* when you call her tonight," Caleb tossed back over his shoulder as he walked away.

"Sure," Jon called after him, hoping he'd actually remember. After trotting down to the office and taking the last two pieces of chicken, Jon walked to the gym and unlocked the supply closet. By then the young players were filtering out of the locker room, shoving one another and making cracks about the "sky blue" walls and "powder puff" benches. Jon could feel himself relax. After a whole day of walking through what seemed to be someone else's life, he could finally feel like he had stepped back into his own—that it hadn't *all* been taken away from him.

❧ ❧ ❧ ❧

Esther cleared her throat one last time and looked over at Steve Forelli, who appeared to be so casual, swiveling back and forth in his chair and clicking his pen as he glanced for the first time at his copy of the script. Catching her eyes on him, he smiled and winked. *He's loving this,* she thought. *He knows how nervous I am and he's absolutely loving it.*

*Smile,* Esther coached herself. Lights glared around her; several people were walking here and there, ignoring the set completely. The gaping window of the control room hung in front of them all, but Esther could not make out anything beyond the tinted glass because of the glare of the brightly lit set. Camera one was evidently having trouble, so camera three was gliding across the smooth floor to take up the central position in the set while the red light above camera two called for Esther to look that direction.

"Five, four, three, two and—"

"Good evening. Tonight I have the pleasure of introducing Esther Branson, who is filling in for Sybil Horn." Steve's voice was so fluid, so professional. Esther was duly impressed.

"Thank you, Steve," she answered warmly. "It's a pleasure to be joining you."

"We all know Esther from the quality stories she's given us as Consumer Reporter at noon. So, Esther, we bid you welcome. Now to our top stories, which tonight include the recent car-jacking . . ."

Esther swallowed hard. She had worked live before but never during peak hours. Funny, she would never have guessed it would have made so much difference to her. The studio itself had not changed. It was simply the knowledge that the viewing audience had grown exponentially beyond what it was at noon. And that the dollars involved for advertising had increased comparably.

Eyeing the TelePrompTer messages superimposed on the camera lens, Esther followed carefully for her script to scroll up onto the screen.

"On the national scene this evening, we have Delia Oliver in New England covering the near tragic, but truly amazing crash of a privately chartered plane that went down just outside of Kennebunk, Maine. We're told that of the twelve passengers on board, only one sustained a minor injury. Delia, what additional information have you been able to obtain?" Esther turned to the blank green screen behind the anchor desk, feigning a conversation with the unfamiliar reporter, responding to her only by the replies heard in the earpiece. Out of the corner of her eye she could see the line of onlookers, just beyond the camera view. Watt stood nearest, watching intently.

"How many crew members were aboard?" Esther questioned.

"As far as is known, there were at least two flight attendants, as well as the pilot and co-pilot, who were also aboard" came the reply.

Esther couldn't help wondering if anyone she knew was watching at just this moment. If only she'd had a chance to set her VCR to tape the show. Maybe Annie would think of it in time. Neal wouldn't be back at his condominium for at least a couple more hours.

*Neal!* She should have called him. He might even be upset that she hadn't. Well, she could only hope that he'd be more proud of her new position than annoyed at her overlooking the call to him.

"Is there any explanation as to why the plane's right engine quit?" she continued her questioning toward the empty screen.

When the first commercial break came, the room around them sprung to life. Someone hurried forward to adjust Esther's collar and flick back one side of her hair. Someone else shoved an edit onto the desk in front of Steve, who frowned and skimmed it briefly, then shuffled it into his stack of printed script. Esther took a moment to eye him carefully.

There was a rhythm between herself and her new co-anchor. Esther was sure she could feel it already. In her limited time on camera, she knew what it was like to work with someone with whom there was no rhythm—no shared sense of timing. Almost as clearly as she could read the screens flashing words in front of her, she felt she could read the tones and inflections of Steve's voice beside her. He was experienced and formal, and she felt herself adjusting to add warmth and sincerity—smiling in agreement with his comments. He, in turn, seemed to be responding well to her—nodding at her dialogue.

In moments they received the signal to begin again. Half an hour finally passed. Then another fifteen minutes. Esther was ready to have the bright lights turned off. It felt as if her hair was beginning to slide loose where a stray curl had been pinned back at the last minute.

The weather forecast was summarized again "for those viewers who joined us late." Then the lead stories were reviewed briefly. Esther read the human-interest offering for the night, then Steve rounded out the evening with a full-length story on a national missing-person search—a youngster who had been abducted late last night from his Chicago suburb—which had been given brief mention several times earlier in the broadcast. Apparently that had been the late addition to Steve's script and all of the information about the event had not even been gathered until the broadcast was already underway. Steve was undaunted and controlled. Esther was awed by his composure.

Finally, it was over. "That was good" was his only comment in Esther's direction. But for her, that was enough. Then horror washed over her—she would have to do it all over again at ten-thirty. The thought almost made her knees buckle.

# Five

*Friday, February 19*

A stiff winter breeze whipped Esther's wool coat against her legs when she finally stepped out of the news station and onto the lighted sidewalk. With one hand on her hat and the other grasping at her coat, she hurried around the corner of the building to where her car was parked. Stopping short, she stared at a dark form in the front seat of her car. It was a man!

*What should I do? Call security? Stay inside the building until he leaves?* She cautiously edged closer, keeping several car widths in between, trying to be certain her eyes weren't playing tricks on her. Then the shadowed man looked up, and Esther fought the urge to flee.

He was opening the door. He was stepping out. Just as she was about to turn and run, it became obvious that the man was Neal. His broad grin seemed to glow in the darkness, even from behind the jacket lapels that he had pulled up around his face to keep out the wind. *My car was locked. How did he get in?*

"You look surprised to see me, sugar. You're white as a ghost."

"I almost fainted, Neal," Esther choked. "How did you unlock the door?"

"Last time I used it I had a key made." He said it simply, as a matter of little consequence. Esther wasn't sure why it bothered her—after all, they were going to be married soon. But, somehow, it seemed underhanded to her. Perhaps the adrenaline still coursing through her veins was making her annoyed when there was no need.

"You don't mind, do you, darlin'?" Neal's arms were going around her, pulling her close to him and shielding her from the wind. "I would have asked first, but I was already making copies of my keys for you. It was easier just to go ahead."

"No, it's all right. I guess I'm tired and grouchy." Esther tucked her face against the warmth of his neck for a brief moment, then backed away. "And cold. I'm very, very cold. Let's go."

Neal guided Esther into the passenger seat, then dashed around and slid in under the steering wheel. "Big day," he grinned at her.

"Unbelievable! I've had so many shocks today I just can't even think straight. Did you get my message?"

Neal was backing out of the parking space, still managing to smile in Esther's direction. He was so obviously pleased with her. "No, I haven't checked my voice mail yet. But what great news! Still, I'm not surprised. I told you it wouldn't be long till you were an anchor. I could see success written all over you from the moment I saw you in Minnesota."

Esther laughed. She hadn't thought about how they had met for so long that it almost seemed like someone else's life. She could still see the battered studio set in Rochester where she had tried so hard to be a good reporter at her first job—usually putting in far more work than was expected, but not always producing a better story or presentation. She'd had so much to learn.

What Neal said was true. The moment she had seen him watching her from behind the cameras, she could tell he was interested in her. Then, when the show was finished, they had been introduced. In her mind, that moment would be suspended for all time . . . his clear blue eyes, the clean cut of his suit, the laugh lines that drew back across his cheeks and around his eyes, making his smile send queer fireworks along her spine. *Did he steal my heart at that very moment*? Certainly, it had not taken him long.

She was only twenty-five then and still in the first job she had gotten after finishing college. For two years she had struggled as a stranger in a lonely city. Then Neal had arrived. Already past thirty and established in a small but impressive executive placement service, he had seemed exciting and powerful. That he had paid her even the slightest bit of attention was still a mystery to Esther, but they had begun dating immediately. Even though Neal's home was in Texas and his business trips to her area lasted only another two months, they found opportunities to see each other. In a way, distance seemed to make the relationship all the more exciting.

Before many months had passed, Neal had begun "helping" her career. It wasn't altogether surprising, since that was what he did professionally in the news industry, but she was flattered that he took the time. She was such a small wheel in the huge media machine, and yet he seemed to expect her to advance. At his insistence, Esther had prepared numerous copies of a tape of clips from her news reporting—her "video resumé" he had called it. Neal was the one who had sent the tapes to stations all across the country. He was the one who felt she had so much potential. He was the one who had encouraged her to spend her carefully guarded money on clothes for interviews. Promoting Esther was important to Neal.

And, of course, she surely would not have gotten her current position had it not been for his persistence. Would she still be back in her small-town station in Minnesota without his help? Looking over at him now, Esther studied his face.

There was a hint of curl showing along the fringes of his short, professional-style haircut, which was always kept impeccably. His clear blue eyes were looking out into the lighted streets. Those eyes shone when they looked at her. That was probably the thing about Neal she enjoyed most—that he truly loved her. She could just watch his face and know that here was a man who thought the world of her, expected her success far more than she herself did, and was entirely intent on seeing her happy and well cared for. It would shine at her in his eyes.

Yes, there were times when Esther had seen Neal become angry—had watched those eyes cloud with something close to rage. But the fierce look had never been directed at her and had always passed quickly. That was another thing about Neal: he always kept himself carefully under control.

"You're quiet, sugar, for someone with so much to tell about her day."

"I'm sorry. I was lost in thought."

"What were you thinking about?"

"Oh, just us. I was remembering what it was like in Minnesota when we were dating. Do you remember all those late phone calls? I can't believe how long we talked. . . ." Esther leaned her head back against the headrest and closed her eyes.

"You had a lot to say—stuck out there in cow town with nobody else around."

"I loved Minnesota! It was quiet and comfortable—and beautiful. If you had come there instead of me coming south, I would have been just thrilled."

"Sure, darlin', but you're forgetting the mountains of snow all winter and the swarms of mosquitoes all summer."

Esther laughed. "Well, I'm happy. I'd go anywhere just to be with you." Neal reached over and gave her hand a squeeze.

Annie was wrong about Neal. Esther felt she had never been happier. Marrying Neal would be her best decision yet.

"About the promotion, Esther."

"Uh-huh?"

"Well, it's really important—especially now—that you're careful to make a good impression."

"What do you mean?"

"Well, you know they fired that other woman because she didn't buckle down. And, well, sometimes you let your ideals get a little too overpowering."

"My ideals?"

"You know, your morals—your beliefs. I love you for it," he was quick to interject. "It makes you who you are, but . . ."

"You want me to blend in?" Esther was a little amused by the conversation.

"Just don't make waves. Make yourself invaluable first, then you can fight for righteousness or whatever. Okay?"

She could just make out his wink at her. Then he smiled broadly. There it was. The smile that could always make her heart skip a beat.

"I'll be good," she conceded, then scooted closer to him and began to stroke the hair along his temple. "I'm too scared I'll breathe the wrong way right now."

"Sugar, you were great. They've got to love you. You make Sybil Horn look like an old gym teacher I once had."

"Neal!"

"Well, you do. You just sit there and glow. But you're smart, too. Anybody watching can see you know your way around the issues. And, darlin', if you're not in a network studio within five years, I'll eat my socks."

Esther couldn't guard herself from Neal's praise. Whatever compliments he lavished her way she always lapped up like a puppy at his feet. But she didn't mind. She was amply convinced that he loved her deeply. What more obvious way to show her than to charm her with every word he said.

It didn't matter, either, that she knew it was his job to

encourage—even flatter—his clients. She'd seen him smooth and charming, completely at ease, as he negotiated the deal of the century over lunch with a business associate. There were always exaggerated compliments involved. But Neal almost always came out ahead. In fact, to Esther's knowledge, the only person who seemed to be cold to such tactics was Annie.

Annie hated flattery. It was probably the trait that bothered her most about Neal. Given enough time to get used to him, Esther was sure that Annie would begin to see in Neal what she herself did—the sensitivity, the tenderness, the trustworthiness. It would just take a little time.

❧ ❧ ❧ ❧

"Mom? It's Jon."

"Jonnie, it's so good to hear your voice." It was late by the time Jon had remembered to call home. He knew that his father would have already gone to bed, but he had taken the calculated risk that his mother would still be awake. They shared the characteristic of enjoying the late-night quiet for catching up on work. "I didn't get you up, did I?"

"No, no. I had some typing to do for the church and it just didn't get done until now."

"What is it you're typing?"

"Oh, just some notes from the board meeting. I volunteered to be church secretary so I could attend the meetings with your dad—and not have to head a committee like I've always done. Well, I had no idea how much work would be involved. But," she sighed, "I *do* still feel involved. In fact, sometimes I think I gave up being in charge of one committee to be involved in *all* of them instead. That wasn't really what I had in mind. Oh, well. How is the center?"

"Good. We trained three more staff and we've got more kids who want to be in the basketball league than we can handle. Classes for job skills and Bible studies fill up a lot more slowly, but we expected that. We've been praying every day, and if basketball works better than other things, at least it's a start."

Jon's mother heard the brooding behind the words. "Numbers aren't the final word, Jonnie. Don't forget about Carl, that man you hired to be a janitor at the center to give him a place to sleep at night. You were so pleased when he checked into an alcohol rehabilitation center after just a few weeks around the people there. You may never know how much difference you made in his life—but you can know you *did* help him to start over. And there's Teresa, and Scott, and Merrill. And there're bound to be so many names that you haven't even mentioned to Dad and me. I know it's hard to see all that now, but don't let yourself believe that you're not making a difference." Her words were drawing courage back to Jon. "Remember, Jonnie . . ."

"I know, Mom." He had heard her repeat the words often enough. "It's not my plan succeeding, it's the people being helped that God really cares about." Jon leaned his head against the receiver, wishing he could have more than just the sound of her voice in the room with him.

"How was your first day home?" There it was. The real question. She'd known from the start that his discouragement came more from the suspension from teaching than from work at the center. This question cut through the pretense and exposed the raw wounds.

"It was hard." He paused, struggling for a way to express what he was feeling. "I feel lost. Like I don't have a place or a role. I'm afraid I'm going to spend the next few weeks making up things to do because I really don't have enough to fill my time. It's as if my life's been put on hold and I'm just watching the clock tick away."

There was stillness as she thought about his words, searching for an answer. They both knew that answers were hard to come by, especially for unfolding events. All they would be able to accomplish was to speculate, and speculation was a very unsatisfying thing. "I love you," she whispered at last.

"I know." His reply was quieter still. For just a moment more, Jon let himself feel the sympathy that hung thick in their silence. Then, drawing a deep breath, he announced, "I'm doing quite a bit of reading, though."

"Oh?"

"Yeah. There's actually a lot more written on the topic of creation from a scientific perspective than I had thought. I'm giving myself a crash course."

"Are you planning to use the information in the hearing?"

"I don't know, but at least I'll have a 'ready defense.' That can't hurt."

"When do they think the hearing will be?"

"It hasn't been set. Denny, our principal, thought it would be at least two or three weeks. But I wouldn't be surprised if it went a little longer than that. I've been told these things have a way of getting bumped further and further back."

"Oh, I hope not. For your sake, I hope it all moves quickly." There was a pause. "I suppose they're not paying you while you're not teaching."

"Actually they are. So I'll be fine." Discussing money with her made Jon feel a little edgy. He was hoping she wouldn't hear it in his voice.

"Well, I know you will be. And I'm glad now that Caleb *is* down there with you. I guess God knew you were going to need him."

"It really helps to have him around. That's for sure."

"As for the hearing, you know how I feel, but I'm going to say it anyway. You aren't a troublemaker. You never were. I know you were just saying what you felt was the truth. So

I know God is in control of this situation and He will be with you every step of the way. We're praying; you know that. And I wanted this chance to remind you of a verse. That's really why I called. I felt so strongly today that this verse is for you. 'Do whatever your hand finds to do, for God is with you.' That's all, Jonnie. Just do what's in front of you, and try not to struggle inwardly. Find your peace with God, and don't let the people around you take it away."

"Thanks, Mom." He closed his eyes. He knew she meant more by her words than she could even express. "I won't forget."

"I love you, son."

"I love you, too."

"I'll call you again in a couple days."

"Okay."

"Good night, then. I'd better get back to work."

"Good night." Jon dropped the receiver softly into its cradle. He felt better, but something in his chest was squeezing tightly. His big black lab, Commodore, leaned up against his leg, and Jon reached an absentminded hand down to scratch behind his ear. It was quiet in the house. Caleb was already asleep, but Jon knew it would be some time before he could settle in himself. Instead, he walked to his desk in the corner of the crowded living room and flipped open the books he had been studying earlier. Pulling out a fresh notebook, he started through the next chapter and launched himself into another theory.

# Six

*Thursday, March 4*

Jon flipped the end of his tie around, hoping this time the knot would look like it should. "Hey, Cale, can you give me a hand?"

Caleb appeared in the doorway, already wearing his coat and looking distraught that Jon was not ready. "Nine-thirty. We've got to be *in the hearing room* at nine-thirty. Not on the sidewalk in front, not in the hallway—in the hearing room. And if we don't get out of here on time, we're not going to have a shot at a parking spot anywhere near the building."

"But you're my brother. You'd drop me off at the door, right?" Jon shot a crooked grin in Caleb's direction.

"Somehow you keep forgetting that genetically I don't owe you diddly." His attempt at hiding his grin failed. "And even if I did drop you at the door, you'd probably never find the right room. Judging by how many books and pages are scattered all over the living room, I'll bet you didn't get any sleep last night. The tie is fine. Just get your notes so we can go."

Silence hung over the car. Jon was both anxious to get the hearing under way and dreading that it was to happen. They had all been amazed when it was scheduled for only two weeks after Jon had left the school.

The hearing room was easy to find but strangely quiet. Jon took a seat at the table in the center of the room, while Caleb chose to sit in the first of the four rows of chairs behind him. There was no one else in sight. Jon checked his watch; they were only ten minutes early. Could they be in the wrong room? Maybe they had gotten the time wrong.

Turning to look at Caleb, Jon leaned over and whispered, "Are you sure we didn't make a mistake? It doesn't seem like they're ready for a hearing." Caleb just shrugged in response.

After a moment or two of waiting, Jon watched a woman with a steno pad enter through the main door and walk toward him. "Are you Jon Shepherd?" she asked formally.

"Yes."

"The hearing has been moved to another room. Could you follow me, please?"

Jon gathered his notebook and jacket to fall in behind, coming moments later to a meeting room off of the main hallway. This time the impending meeting was obvious. Two men and a woman, apparently members of the school board, sat on one side of a long oak table. Beside them, Jon saw Denny Trent, seated and smiling.

"Good morning," Denny offered jovially.

"Hi." Jon took a seat on the opposite side of the table. After looking around for a less visible spot, Caleb slipped into a chair beside Jon.

The man who seemed to be leading the meeting reached across the table and extended his hand to Jon, and then also shook hands with Caleb. After a few words of greeting, he launched into the business at hand. "Well, we're not going to be very formal here, Jon. We don't expect this to take long, but we thought we'd at least be comfortable and out of the way here in a meeting room. Everyone on the board agreed that there was no need to make a production out of this hearing. I'm sure you agree."

Jon watched the speaker's face carefully, not sure whether he was seeing genuine friendship or just patronage. "This is fine," he nodded, turning to Denny for some clue as to how to interpret the change. Denny just smiled back confidently.

"How about a little coffee before we begin? The table in the corner behind you has cups and a coffeepot if you're interested. Or we can scare you up some iced tea, too."

"No, thank you. I'm fine."

"Okay, then. I guess we'll just jump right in. My name is Henley Brinkner and I'm chairman of the school board for . . . what is it now? . . . I guess this is my third year." Jon watched as the man shuffled the papers in front of him absentmindedly.

"I've talked with Denny, who has stood behind you one hundred percent. He's been quick to uphold you as a fine teacher—sincere, principled, and reliable." For a moment he paused and chuckled to himself. "And he says the kids like you, too. Sitting where I do, I don't get to see many teachers in a hearing who have all those endorsements tagged on." Denny was smiling again. The lady with the steno pad was jotting notes in a casual manner.

"So let's just cut to the bottom line here, Jon. You've been away from your classes for about two weeks. We hurried this hearing along simply because we—all of us here—want you right back in your classroom where you belong. And I don't see any reason why there needs to be any more excitement stirred up over something so small."

*The school board isn't going to make an issue of this case*, Jon realized with relief. Apparently there would be no serious inquiry. This was not going to be a big deal, after all. Jon could feel himself relaxing into his chair.

"We can all respect your religious convictions. I'm a Christian myself—pretty much born and raised in the oldest church in my part of the city. So I can see how a little religious fervor could get you carried away. And I understand how what you heard Sunday morning could kind of slip into a school discussion. It's never affected your teaching before, and we're all willing to believe that it's not going to get tangled up in classroom lessons again. Why, from what I understand about *this* situation, all we have to do is keep you away from the science curriculum." Henley Brinkner was leaning back in his chair and chuckling to Denny. Denny was sending him back a broad smile, both of them certain that they would be back in their cars in less than twenty minutes.

Slowly, the skin on the back of Jon's neck began to bristle.

"All we need from you, Jon, is this: agree not to go into your personal religious philosophy in the classroom, and stick to teaching what has been approved by the board. As long as we can take your word back to the rest of the school board that we've reached an agreement, I don't see why you can't be back in your classroom in time to finish that Civil War study that Denny said you were anxious to teach."

Brinkner and Denny exchanged nods.

Jon looked down at the floor, crushing down the feelings that were rising in him and quickly sifting through the words to understand exactly what was being said. *Oh, Father, don't let me make a mistake here*, he prayed fervently. *Put the right words in my mouth. I need you now.*

"Excuse me, Mr. Brinkner," he interrupted cautiously.

"Henley, please. Call me Henley."

"Okay—Henley—I guess I just want to understand what you're saying. You expect me to keep my 'personal religious philosophy' out of the classroom?" Denny's eyes were beginning to squint, and his averted gaze told Jon that the man had an inkling of what was coming next. He'd seen Jon dig in his heels in meetings before, but Jon bet he had never dreamed it would happen here.

"Why, separation of church and state, clear and simple." The smile on Henley Brinkner's face took on a sculpted look.

"So we can put 'In God We Trust' on our money but not

in our schools? You said that you're a Christian. Do you mean to tell me that you leave your 'religious philosophy' at the door of your office before stepping inside?" Now even Caleb was staring with wide eyes.

"You can *believe* anything you want—but you don't *teach* what's not approved."

"Do you *believe* what's being taught?"

"If you're referring to evolution, that's not the point."

"How can that not be the point?"

Henley Brinkner sat back in his chair to collect his thoughts. Jon leaned forward, waiting for his response.

"Jon, you're young. And when you're young it seems like every battle is worth the fight. Okay, I'll answer your question honestly. Do I believe in evolution? No, I can't say that I do. And I'm not sure many of our teachers really believe it all. But if we don't teach evolution, what do we teach about the origin of the world? We can't just say God did it and call that science class. Let's bottom line this, son. What is it that you're trying to do here?"

Jon hoped with all of his heart he could get this man—this whole board—to understand. "Mr. Brinkner—Henley—I don't have a 'bottom line' because I don't have an agenda. I walked into this thing blindly and I haven't made any plans. But it seems that you're asking me to keep my convictions to myself and basically suppress any idea other than what's in the text." His voice softened. "My religious convictions aren't just what I think, they're also who I am. My belief in God just can't be sectioned off into a closet while I'm teaching. It's the best part of my life—it's what has instilled in me a heart for teaching. My belief in God makes me see each student as important and makes me want to meet their needs, one at a time.

"And my belief in God has shaped every study I've *ever* done in history. Every interpretation I have has passed through my own belief that God has guided human history from creation to the present. How can you ask me to suppress that? It's not possible."

"I think we're losing sight of the issue here, Jon. It's really not as big as all of that. We just need you to keep your interpretations out of the lessons. Like I already said, I think our problem here is solved if we just stop shuffling our teaching staff around so much—and keep you out of science class. And I'm willing to call it case closed on that alone." Then his eyes came up to face off with Jon's. "But I've got to be able to go back to the parents and students who brought the complaint and assure them that there will be no more problems."

Jon hesitated for a moment, quickly grappling for what to say next. "Mr. Brinkner, I don't believe I said anything that was out of line. I questioned a theory that was printed in a junior high textbook as scientific fact, even though there remain major holes in the theory itself. Then I presented to the students—being very careful to point out that the ideas I was presenting were also theories—that there was a neglected realm of thought."

"But it's not science, Mr. Shepherd," Brinkner said abruptly, all pretense of friendliness gone now from his voice.

Jon flipped open his notebook as he responded. "I'm afraid that there are many scientists who would disagree. Did you know that Isaac Newton, who is often called the 'father of modern science,' believed in a literal six days of creation and a worldwide flood and that he wrote a number of papers actually defending both interpretations? That's not in the textbook. And I have this great quote from Wernher von Braun, who was at one time a director of NASA. Listen to this. He wrote, 'Manned space flight is an amazing achievement, but it has opened for mankind thus far only a tiny door for viewing the awesome reaches of space. An outlook through this peephole at the vast mysteries of the universe should only confirm our belief in the certainty of its Creator.'

I'm sorry, Mr. Brinkner. I have to disagree with you. Many intelligent people, including leading scientists, have no problem linking science and belief in God."

Henley Brinkner set down his papers and clasped his hands over them. "We don't have time to debate with you, son. Let me define what you're saying: you are unwilling to submit to the policy of this board by refraining from interjecting religious beliefs into classroom teachings."

"I'm saying that I'm not willing to teach evolution as fact, even if the board has declared it to be so. I'm saying that the students have a right to hear an alternative theory, and we have the responsibility to present it to them. I'm saying that I'm not willing to apologize because I don't believe I've done anything wrong."

"I'm sorry it came to this, Mr. Shepherd. I was hoping to avoid further difficulties in this case, but if you're going to force the issue I'm afraid we're going to have to reschedule so that we can have a full-fledged hearing. That *would* be unfortunate. Is that what you're choosing?"

"I'm sorry that's an inconvenience. Please believe me. That was never my intention. But I guess in a way, I feel differently than you do. I find myself quite interested in having a *hearing*. I guess I feel I have some comments that need to be heard."

Mr. Brinkner rose from his seat. "I just hope you understand the direction that you're heading." This time, there was no hand of goodwill offered across the table.

Jon and Caleb gathered their belongings in silence and started away from the meeting room.

❧ ❧ ❧ ❧

The new schedule of having the morning to herself but remaining at work until late took a while for Esther to embrace. Her body simply refused to sleep in and then complained about being kept up so late. There were so many other elements of the new job, though, that Esther thoroughly enjoyed—especially being more involved in the development process for all of the news pieces instead of just one or two segments. This also gave her more confidence and genuine interest when reading the stories on air. And when it came to introducing other reporters, Esther's days in their position were so recent and her sympathetic feelings so fresh that she always did her best to build them up and make them look good on camera.

Steve proved to be easy to work with. Off camera he had an easy manner, with a quick smile and a very dry wit. On camera he was mostly business, smiling in return to laughter around him but rarely instigating it. However, Esther had been correct in suspecting that they would work well together. Letters from viewers poured in, all lauding the station's choice of Esther for co-anchor. They called her personable, warm, compassionate, trustworthy, and "a rose among thorns."

Esther supposed the letter must mean that the other thorns were their weather forecaster, Joe Wertheim, and their sportscaster, Gabe LeClaire. Joe was older, reaching retirement age, and very well respected in all circles. He had been in weather forecasting for many, many years, but had truly made a name for himself by pursuing all the most current information and newest technology. In fact, Joe had dabbled with inventions for meteorological devices for years on his own time, and there was an unsubstantiated rumor that he held at least one patent. Joe was highly intelligent, friendly, and just a little arrogant.

Gabe LeClaire embodied sports to Esther. An ex-football player, Gabe was well known to fans across the U.S., having played for the Florida Gators. He had supposedly shown much promise when he entered professional sports but had been injured in his third year. Gabe was broad and black and bold in every way. Often the entire studio would ring with the deep, hearty tones of his laughter, and in Esther's view the studio could use a little more excitement anyway. The viewing audience must have agreed, because Gabe was commended on every side for his work. In all, Esther found she was pleased with each of the men with whom she shared the spotlight.

However, Watt Shreve proved to be just as difficult as Esther had expected. He did not hesitate to make rude and condescending remarks behind people's backs or directly to them. Editorial meetings led by him were unpleasant affairs. Esther could tell that most of her fellow employees had as little respect for him as she did, but no one was bold enough to counter his ideas. It was a shame. As Esther looked at each face around the meeting table, she was convinced that much of the creativity and insight they represented was being wasted simply because of Watt's oppressive management style. As the new kid on the block, she was not about to stir up trouble. Even without Neal's warning, she would have certainly held her tongue.

Neal. He had inadvertently provoked a difficult set of decisions for Esther. She loved the new house. There was no denying that. From its perfect location, wooded site, and wonderful size to its beautifully detailed carpentry. But what was she to do about the house when the wedding was still months away?

Esther was grateful that Neal had been noble about the whole thing. At first he had been greatly disappointed that she was still refusing to live in the house with him. She encouraged him to move in himself, saving the rent on his own condo and "getting things ready." Neal would not hear of it. In short order, he had made arrangements for Esther herself to move into the house.

Now the movers were scheduled to pack her belongings at ten o'clock—the earliest available slot—and she had been busy for three days boxing the items that needed extra care.

The move itself hadn't come at a good time for Esther. With the excitement of the new job, she was already feeling anxious and unsettled. But Neal was adamant that she should take the house, so Esther did her best to shove aside her misgivings. *How can I complain about being given the home of my dreams? Surely I'm not as selfish as that!*

So Esther found herself in a mad scramble to be ready for the movers. When they arrived and began filling boxes of their own, Esther prowled from room to room, looking over each man's shoulder by turn and giving instructions. Never before had she paid someone else to pack her things. If she had had the time, she would certainly have preferred to do it herself.

In less than two hours they were finished and the truck was pulling away from where it had sprawled in front of her apartment building. Esther placed the last of her plants on the newspaper in the trunk of her car and slid in behind the wheel. *What am I doing? I have to be at work in less than four hours—hardly enough time to watch the movers unload.* She wouldn't have time to unpack even one box before she'd have to leave for work.

The few scattered furnishings and boxes mocked the empty, hollow spaces of the big house. Once the moving men had gathered together their furniture pads and pulled away from the driveway, Esther was sure she could even hear the echo of her own breathing.

*Maybe it wouldn't be so bad to let Neal move in, too.* It seemed she was the only one who showed the least amount of concern about the potential housing arrangement, anyway. If it hadn't been for her churched upbringing, she would probably have shrugged it off like everyone else.

But no, she could never regret the values instilled in her as a child. In fact, she clung to them tenaciously. True, she was no longer in her own hometown. True, there were no neighbors around to discuss her private affairs, but that had never been what had motivated her parents to conform, nor what had made Esther hold to the small-town morals. It was the security of knowing right from wrong. It was the constancy and stability it gave her in a world that had changed almost more than she could bear from when she was a child. And in a vague way, Esther was aware of something more—some unnamed reason her Christian upbringing seemed to be an intricate part of her being.

*In fact, wouldn't it be nice if Neal and I began married life by joining and regularly attending a local church?* She'd have to bring up the subject when she talked to him tomorrow night. She was sure he would share her enthusiasm.

"Well, I'm in." Esther had stopped by her desk after the day's editorial meeting. She had only time enough for a brief call to Neal.

"Great, darlin'! How does it feel?"

"I don't know. It'll take some getting used to, I guess. There's just so much space in that house."

"Isn't it perfect! I can hardly wait to see what you've done to it."

Esther pictured the piles of boxes and the large, colorless rooms surrounding them. "I haven't done anything at all. I still have to unpack, but right now I can't even begin to think about what a big job it'll be to decorate."

"Well, think of it as a blank canvas. I'm sure you'll have it pretty as a picture in no time, sugar. I know that much about you."

"Sure, Neal." Esther did not share his enthusiasm at all. "I've got to go now."

"Okay. Hey, Esther?"

"Uh-huh?"

"How did the meeting go today? Your voice sounds a little tense. There wasn't a problem, was there?"

"No, it's not that. I mean, yes, Watt's as big a jerk as ever, but it's really more just moving into the house. I'll feel better once it's all settled."

"Okay. Well, I'll see you tonight, darlin'."

"Yeah, I'll see you tonight."

❧ ❧ ❧ ❧

Jon moved stoically through the afternoon routine he had built at the youth center. It wasn't that he was deep in thought, but his mind seemed to have shut off since the hearing that morning. The looming questions that had been raised refused to even crystallize in his head. Mechanically, he coached and cleaned and finished up some lesson plans for the following week's Bible study.

When at last they were home and Caleb had gone to bed, Jon pulled a chair up beside his desk and put his head down on his arms. Commodore nuzzled up beside him in an attempt to draw him out of his pensive mood, but Jon didn't even notice. Turning around twice, the dog lay down beside his chair to wait.

*Lord*, Jon's heart cried out as he pressed his face into his hands, *I don't know what I'm doing. I don't know if I'm starting a meaningless fight over semantics, or if I'm really being led into taking a stand. I just need to know—for sure. If this is what you want from me, you know I'll do it, but I'm just not sure. And I don't want—I can't—drag myself, my family, and the people I work with through a meaningless fight over words. But I won't quit if this is really part of a spiritual battle. I need to know, Father. I need to know.*

Emotion surged up inside Jon, and for the first time in years he wept. Commodore whined softly at his feet, eyebrows drawn forward in concern.

For the next few hours Jon prayed, thumbing through his

worn Bible for guidance. There was no other way. This was not a position he was willing to take unless he was very convinced that he had been called upon to do so.

In the morning, Jon felt a hand on his shoulder, shaking insistently. Groggily, he realized he must have fallen asleep at his desk.

"Jon." It was his brother's voice. "Jon, wake up."

With blurred eyes Jon struggled to look up at Caleb.

"I just got the newspaper. Look." Caleb slid the paper across the desk to Jon and pointed to the lower corner where the contents of the various sections were listed.

Forcing his eyes to focus, Jon read, "School News: Local Teacher Takes on School Board Over Teaching Creation." Gradually, the meaning of the words came to him. It was no longer going to be a private battle. Jon raised his eyes to survey Caleb's reaction.

"I think you've got a fight on your hands, big brother."

Jon studied him. His mind was whirling now. "Do I? Should I?"

Caleb smiled down toward him. "If not you, then who?"

# Seven

*Saturday, March 6*

Esther spent Saturday getting settled in the new house. Annie came around lunchtime to see the place and lend a hand for a little while.

"It's big." Annie had always been very direct.

"Neal says it won't be long until we need a house this size, so it's better to get it now instead of moving again in a few years."

"Well, it looks like the 'Sugar Man' has turned into your 'Sugar Daddy.' Can you guys really afford this place?"

Esther scowled, then answered honestly. "I guess. With Neal's income and my raise, we can make the payments. It doesn't leave much of a budget for furniture, though. I feel like I'm living in a castle and sleeping on the floor."

"Well, our little cottage is about the size of your drawbridge. Is it any wonder we can afford to furnish it?"

"Oh, Annie. Your house is great. It was such a good idea to build a duplex and rent out the other side."

"Yeah, well, it works for me and Max. Anyhow, there's always a bright side—I've got a whole pile of things in my garage that I know where to store now." Annie grinned, tossing the box she had finished unpacking into the hallway.

It was difficult for Esther to let Annie go back home; the

house had been so much more enjoyable with her as company. As she watched Annie's little car zip away, her heart sank. *Alone again.*

Moving into the living room, Esther flopped down onto the floor and picked up the closest distraction. It was a photo album, ready to be lined up with the others on the lowest of the built-in shelves next to the fireplace.

Opening to the first page, Esther browsed through the familiar pictures from college. Here was her first dorm room, and her first roommate. She smiled at the antics, from practical jokes on each other to last-minute cramming sessions for exams and at the few pictures of Andy Gray visiting from her hometown. Esther had enjoyed those days, though they felt very distant to her now. When the pictures of her second year at college began, Esther closed the album. She never looked through that part anymore. It held too many painful reminders.

Instead, she picked up the next album and opened to her first pictures of Annie. Annie had been her roommate during her third and fourth years of college. They had started out together in the dorm, and then Annie had quickly talked Esther into sharing an apartment off campus with two other girls for the second semester.

That's when college really began to get exciting for Esther. Annie was determined to attend any and all school events—every basketball game, every choir performance, and every workshop where the speaker looked interesting—or at least attractive and male. They went to parties and other social events, like sledding in the winter and swimming at the beach long before it was warm enough. Somehow, in between all the social events, Esther had found time to study and pull good grades. But Annie had taught her how to have fun—and for Esther, it couldn't have come at a better time in her life.

Each page in the album showed the flaming redhead smiling and laughing, the green eyes sparkling even in the photographs. This was Annie in her glory days, carefree and wild. Esther laughed at the thought of how they had teased each other. Annie's maiden name had been Appel—which had quickly become "Apple" to most of her friends. With her red hair and freckles, Annie seemed to suit the image well. From there it was a short jump to all sorts of nicknames, but the one that had stuck was "Juicy." And Annie had remained "Juicy" until she and Esther began working together. After that, they had agreed not to keep acting like college students—and more specifically—not to use the old pet names.

When she had come to the last page of the album and closed the cover, Esther felt oddly depressed. She remembered what it had been like saying good-bye to her old college friends and moving to the new job in Minnesota. Even though it was a dream job, which she had gotten with much help from the references her professors had given her, it had been a step into one of the loneliest times of her life. And until she had met Neal, there really were no photos, because she hadn't done anything worth taking a picture of.

Esther slid the albums carefully onto the shelf, then forced herself to leave behind her gloomy thoughts and finish setting up the new house.

Even when all of her possessions had been displayed to the best of her ability, the furnishings and decor were skimpy for the grand scale of the home itself. Esther sighed as she placed her stack of eight plates onto the freshly lined kitchen shelf. They looked so lonely. In fact, sitting in the center of the wide shelf, they seemed to personify the way she was feeling. Would she ever feel comfortable in the big house?

Neal arrived in the late afternoon to survey her work. He was pleased but could not hide the fact that he also noticed the lack of furnishings.

"Do you think that—maybe—this house is *too* big?" Esther finally offered her question while they were sitting on the couch watching a video together. Turning away from the television to look at Neal frankly, she watched his face for a reaction.

"No, no—oh, it might feel that way now, but, darlin', just think of the entertaining we can do. Once we've had a chance to get a new dining room suite and I've added my living room furniture, it'll look *really* good."

"I guess." Then Esther remembered the late-morning visit she had had before Annie dropped in. "Neal, the lady from next door stopped by earlier. She didn't come in. She just wanted to introduce herself and say hi. She seemed very nice."

"See there, you fit in already." Neal patted Esther's leg, then turned back toward the television.

"Her name is Sandy Doyle, and her husband is Lewis. They only moved into their house a couple months ago. They're from the East coast."

"What does he do for a living?"

"I don't think she said. She did say something about a transfer, but I don't really remember. She also said they're expecting a baby in about six months. It'll be their first."

"That's nice."

Esther sat for a moment or two more looking at Neal in the flickering light of the television picture. "Neal, I have a question."

He frowned slightly at being interrupted again but turned toward Esther.

"I've been thinking about how nice it would be to join a church. Tomorrow is Sunday, and it would be a great chance to try that big one we pass on Maple Street right at the entrance to our subdivision."

Neal paused before he answered. "What got you thinking about that all of a sudden?"

"Oh, planning the wedding, moving into a house—our house. Even hearing Sandy Doyle talking about having a baby. It just seems like we're settling down and that going to church again would be a good thing." Neal was clearly losing interest; Esther could see it in his eyes. "And just think of the new people we could meet. We'd have friends nearby. It would feel like home."

"I don't know, darlin'. Maybe we can go sometime, but I've got a client to see tomorrow. And besides, Sunday is my only day to sleep in—but we'll try it sometime."

After the movie was over, Esther walked Neal to the door and leaned into his arms for a few moments. He brushed his cheek against her hair. "I'll call tomorrow when I'm done with my meeting. I think I can still get tickets for the dinner theater, sugar, if you're interested."

"That would be nice."

Neal kissed her nose playfully. "What are your plans for tomorrow?"

"I don't really have any. I've already unpacked everything I own. I guess I could get some ironing done, and maybe read a little." She decided to broach the earlier subject one more time. "Neal, would you mind if I went to that church, to check it out?"

"Of course not. If you'd like to go, that's fine with me." Neal chuckled. "See, I'm easy to get along with."

"Good night, Neal. I love you."

"Good night, darlin'."

❧ ❧ ❧ ❧

Sunday morning dawned cold and miserable with a misty rain. For a moment or two, Esther had struggled with whether or not she still wanted to go to the church service. After all, Neal wouldn't be with her. *What will people think of Neal if I start attending without him? They'll assume he's not interested. Perhaps I'll wait until we can go together.*

But no. Esther had decided to ignore all of her rationalizations and just go. She could almost hear her father's voice saying, "It doesn't matter what the weatherman says. We're going to church, and that's that." If he had still been alive, would he have questioned Esther about neglecting attendance for so many years?

And in the end, the service was nice. The music was upbeat. The young pastor was sincere and excited about preaching. The people were friendly, and several made the effort to chat for a moment with Esther. It was a much larger church than Esther had been used to, but it was welcoming.

In a strange way, though, it made Esther feel like a child on her first day of school—wide-eyed and uncomfortable. She had been absent for so many years that "church" had become foreign to her. The familiar hymnals were left closed in their racks on the back of each pew. Instead, an overhead projector illuminated the words to choruses that Esther had never heard before, and for which there was no music to read. It was difficult to stand silently and listen to voices all around her lifting in song. Singing had been one of the things that Esther had enjoyed most about church.

Even the instruments had changed. The mellow sounds of a church organ had been replaced with the rhythms of a keyboard, drums, and several men playing guitars. It reminded Esther more of a concert performance than Sunday morning worship.

But it *was* nice. Esther wouldn't have denied that. In and of itself, Esther enjoyed the music—but it did not bring back the familiar feelings she had been seeking out. In fact, along with the music, the entire rhythm of the service seemed to have changed. People were speaking out from their seats to make comments during the announcements and chirping in during the prayer. Laughter filled the room from time to time, and after the special music was sung by a duet of teenage girls, the entire congregation applauded. Esther's home church had never broken the formal air that governed it on

Sunday morning. When she climbed back into her car and drove home along the wet streets, she had already decided not to attend again until Neal would join her. *Hopefully, he'll have a free Sunday morning in the not-too-distant future. Perhaps if I'm not all alone I could enjoy the service more.*

❧ ❧ ❧ ❧

"I have a prayer request." Jon stood in his pew looking around at the familiar faces of the inner-city congregation, searching for words. "Most of you know that I've been suspended from teaching. And some of you know that I had a hearing on Friday morning about my situation." The faces were all watching Jon intently. "They—the school board—were going to keep the whole thing low-key. It was pretty obvious they were wishing it would just go away so they wouldn't have to deal with the issue." Jon spoke the words like an apology. "But the more I pray about it, the more I see how wrong it is to give in." Here he took a deep breath, glancing down at his hands sliding nervously back and forth on the back of the bench in front of him.

"So I guess my situation has changed. There's going to be a formal hearing now. And I don't know if any of you noticed that the story was written up in the school section of Friday's paper, but I'm afraid the press may have a field day with this.

"I'm asking for prayer for two things. First of all, right now I'm convinced that this is a battle I need to fight. But I am concerned for the people around me. I know these kinds of things can be very uncomfortable—and if it were just me, I wouldn't worry about it—but it's my family and the other teachers at work. Some of them are Christians, too, and I don't want them to get any fallout from these hearings.

"And then, there's the bottom line. We've gotten so far from what the Bible teaches in every aspect of education today that I'm really stretching to find support around me. People I've had a chance to talk to just don't understand the issue here at all. So let me try to state it now for you. I *don't* propose that schools stop teaching evolution—that's not going to happen and it's not what I'm after. I *am* saying that my offering a creation science theory in addition to the evolutionary theory in a public school setting was not a breach of people's rights. And I'm willing to go to the mat to defend my convictions on this issue.

"Now, I know I'm getting long-winded here—but then, I'm a teacher, right? I guess I should close with an essay question." Laughter rippled encouragingly. "Instead, I'm going to just ask each of you to search your hearts on my behalf. Pray that God will send me support so I don't go off on my own crusade. I really need to be sure I'm not making costly mistakes when I'm going to be getting public attention."

Jon glanced around him again. Faces had turned downward. People were contemplating his words. "Well, that's all. Thanks." As he took his seat, an older man seated behind Jon placed a hand on his shoulder and gave it a quick squeeze. Jon smiled back at the friendly face, and the service resumed.

# Eight

*Friday, March 26*

For the past five weeks Esther had gathered the confidence that experience on the television set brings. Viewers watched her become less and less timid about adding to the newsroom banter. Esther felt the most comfortable poking fun with Gabe, perhaps because when the cameras were turned off, his personality changed the least.

The news itself remained the most interesting part of the job for Esther. When she read stories, it was with her whole heart, and the emotion she offered was not contrived or insincere. Esther knew this. And it was her conviction that she would remain in front of the camera only as long as what she presented was truly a part of who she was—and never that she was merely acting the part.

Watt, on the other hand, had no interest in what was actually happening in the news. He cared only for how it affected their show. Esther was appalled by some of his comments, spoken with such coldness.

"Do we know any more about that Humphrey baby? People keep wanting us to give updates, but I think we need to let it die. It's old news. There are better stories."

"You mean, let the story die, not the baby, right?" Gabe said sarcastically, looking a little offended by the comment.

"Yeah, whatever," Watt had answered.

Not only did Esther suspect that Watt had stopped seeing that the news affected real people, but there were times she was afraid he would purposely engineer a situation to create a better angle. Esther shuddered at the thought. Working with Watt, watching him fuss and carry on at the slightest mistake by people around him, was clearly what she liked least about the anchor desk.

"Okay, Chris. Give me your ideas for handling that schoolteacher piece."

Esther's mind snapped to attention. She was aware of the impending hearing. The story had been discussed before but had been rejected by Watt as unnewsworthy.

"Well, all the other stations are planning to run a segment updating the story and giving the date set for the public hearing. I don't think anyone else has an interview yet. Those are pretty hard to come by on this story. The teacher is hard to find and the school board is being very tight-lipped."

"What about us trying for an interview with the teacher? If one of the office staff has connections, we might be able to get an exclusive," Steve suggested.

"I don't see the need." Watt seemed determined to play down the story.

"It could get him into the spotlight and make him more real—less of a fanatic," Steve pressed.

*And if all of the other stations are covering it, won't we look uninformed?* Once again, Esther found herself biting her lip to keep from expressing her opinion.

"No," Watt stated firmly. Then in a flash his expression changed and he turned to Esther, as if he'd read her mind. "Branson, this is a good story for you. It's that human-interest fluff. And in a few weeks, once they've nailed this guy and shown him to be the nut he is, we'll get back to the real stories. Yeah, from now on, this assignment is yours. Any on-air updates will come from you."

Esther tried to hide her astonishment at Watt's sudden change. She looked quickly at Chris, who merely shrugged noncommittally and appeared relieved at the thought of handing over the story. Watt was testing her, she was certain.

"As for tonight, we'll mention it after the second weather update. Branson, give the hearing date, because it's public and we're responsible for that, but don't put the station out on a limb by taking sides."

That was all he would concede.

The night's newscast came and went without incident, in comfortable routine. Esther gave the brief, facts-only piece about the schoolteacher, Jon Shepherd, wondering silently as she read the script what sort of man put his career on the line to stand for such seemingly outdated beliefs. Turning the segment over to Steve, Esther's thoughts flew back to the night Neal stressed that she stifle her own stiff morals, now that she had attained the coveted anchor position.

Pushing aside the uncomfortable direction her thoughts had taken, Esther relaxed into her chair and stretched as the cameras were turned off. Turning to smile at Gabe, she was going to make a pert remark in his direction in answer to his ribbing her on air but was interrupted by a studio aide. "Miss Branson, you have a message."

Esther rose to receive the note. *Who would be calling this late at night?* Neal was on a business trip and had warned her that he would be difficult to reach until the next afternoon. Though she wouldn't have been able to explain why, Esther waited until she was back in her office before reading the note.

"10:43 Call Received From: Trudy Gray, Cold Mill, Nebraska. Message: Death in the Gray family. Please call your mother's home for details."

Esther went white. The Grays—Andy's family. They had been Esther's next-door neighbors while she was growing up—almost an extension of her own family. Mr. and Mrs.

Gray themselves were not very old. So there must have been an accident. But who was killed? Esther thought about kind Mrs. Gray—her weary face but her gentle words. She thought of Mr. Gray's cheerful whistle and his cantering step as he walked down Elm Street to his job in the post office. Then she pictured the children as they had been before she left Cold Mill for college.

Andy, the oldest, had been Esther's best friend—the boy next door. Together they had grown up from preschool through senior high. It was to Andy that Esther had confided her deepest crushes and her biggest heartaches. And it was with Andy that she had shared the best times of her childhood. There was not a flicker of fear allowed into Esther's heart that it was Andy who had been killed. She would have felt it. Yes, she was certain she would have somehow known. She could not possibly have grown so distant from her hometown and the people in it.

Following Andy there were three younger sisters. It made Andy perfectly suited to understand Esther so well. The twins, Belinda and Bonnie, were right on Andy's heels—less than a year and a half space between them. *No wonder Mrs. Gray always looked so tired.*

Muriel was the youngest. She had been born several years after the others—a bonus child, as Mr. Gray had liked to call her. Esther's heart felt sick as she thought about each of the family members. *Maybe it isn't the immediate family. Maybe it's a relative.* Esther dreaded making the call home, but just the same she dialed her mother's number.

"Mom? It's Esther."

"Esther. Oh, Esther! Did you hear about the Grays' loss?"

"I got a message about a death in their family." Esther could not force herself to phrase the question that was really on her heart. "What happened?" she managed to utter past the lump squeezing her throat.

"It's so awful. It was an accident. The whole family is in shock. Oh, Esther, if only you were here. You could be such a comfort to them now. If only you hadn't moved away. You need to come home, Esther. You have to come home and be with us. Please . . ."

"Mom! Mom, you have to tell me what happened. What accident? Who—who died?"

"Oh, my baby, don't you know? It was Andy! Andy was killed in a horrible car crash!" Sobs followed. Esther stood in silence, letting the telephone receiver drop away from her ear and rest on her shoulder. Her mind went numb. It must be a mistake. Somehow there had been a terrible mistake. And then only one thought would come to Esther. As soon as possible, she would fly home.

❧ ❧ ❧ ❧

Once again, Jon was slumped over his desk late into the night. For the last few hours he had been absorbing information from another book, this one detailing the Hydroplate Theory, which he had tried to explain in class—that the earth's strata had been formed during the worldwide flood and the ensuing cataclysms while plates of the earth shifted on a massive scale. The book had everything Jon had been searching for: charts, diagrams, satellite photos of land formations that seemed to support the theory, and much more. Obviously, years of solid scientific evaluation had gone into the book.

By now, he had read other books which proposed even more ideas. Some claimed an old earth and theistic evolution. Jon's head was filled with ideas that he only halfway understood. How would he know which to believe? Then a new thought struck him.

He had asked for counselors. Why not find someone who was closest to the issue, who had been able to hear all of the arguments for and against the literal biblical interpretation of the world's origin? Flipping to the last pages, he found just what he was looking for: the list of researchers who had contributed to the information in the book. Here was a list of possible allies. Jon would print off a letter requesting assistance in his struggle and send it to each of the scientists on the research list. Surely, there would be one or two who would be willing to advise Jon. At least it was worth a try.

Wasting no time, he scribbled the name and address of each scientist onto eleven envelopes. Then, clicking on the power to his PC, he gathered his thoughts to transcribe them into a letter. The hearing was set for Friday, April 16th—three weeks away. That should be enough time to hear back from one or two people to whom he was sending letters.

*Father, thank you. This book and the names—they're just what I needed. Please prepare these people to read my letter. Make it something that draws them into helping me. Give me the right words.*

Jon worked on his letter for a full two hours, stuffing and licking the last of the envelopes well after three o'clock in the morning. Then he collapsed onto the couch with the TV remote in his hand, hoping to slow down his thoughts and adrenaline. In no time he was asleep, the television still blinking away in its corner.

Jon closed the front door with a thud and headed toward the mailbox. He was impatient. The letters he had written during the night had not even begun their journey, and he was already frustrated by the length of time that would be involved.

Padding forward in his slippers toward the driveway, he stopped short in disbelief. *My car!* It was covered with smears and stains. Egg yolks dripped from the bumpers and streaked across the windows. Broken shells were plastered across the hood and sides. Even the roof was smeared with glop.

"Caleb," Jon called from where he stood. "Caleb, quick!"

Caleb was at the door instantly. "What? What is it? What's wrong?"

"My car!" Jon could feel his voice warble weakly.

Caleb scurried past where Jon stood frozen on the sidewalk. "No way." His mouth dropped open and his eyes surveyed the damage carefully. He reached his hand out to the vehicle. "No way!" Then he turned back around to see Jon's reaction.

"Who?" Jon whispered. "Who would do this?"

"I have no idea."

"We'll never get it off. It's dried on. The paint is ruined. Who would do this?"

"We'd better call the police."

"What?" Jon's mind was unable to understand.

"You need to file a police report. This is because of all the news coverage about the hearing. Whoever did this is telling you to back off. This is a threat, Jon. Call the police." Caleb's voice was rising as he spoke.

Jon looked over at the car one more time and then back at Caleb.

"Okay," he conceded. "I'll call."

Jon and Caleb sat together waiting on the front lawn for just over two hours before a police car approached. The officer parked his car and stepped onto the street, pausing to gather his notebook and pen from inside his vehicle.

Once he was closer he offered a hand toward the shaken brothers. "I'm Officer Christy. Which of y'all is the vehicle's owner?"

"I'm Jon Shepherd. It's my car."

Officer Christy stepped closer to it and flicked off a piece of shell. "Did a good job."

Caleb turned to look at Jon, who rolled his eyes in return.

The policeman circled the car slowly, assessing the damage and then returning to stand beside Jon.

"Who's mad enough at you to do this?"

Caleb answered on Jon's behalf. "He's been in the news lately. He's a schoolteacher and was suspended over what he taught during one of his classes. There's going to be a hearing. I'm sure it has to do with that."

"You thet teacher who's been preachin' the Bible in class?"

Jon recoiled and answered in a guarded tone. "I just offered an opinion that was different than the book."

Officer Christy laughed. "Well, I've got no beef with you, sir. You do's you see fit. But I don't suppose you'll get very far. No matter, no matter. You do what ya want. But you're bound to get more than an eggin' out of it."

"Are you going to report this?" Caleb wanted a bottom line.

"Sure, sure. I'll write ya out a report. An' it'll be on file if you ever need it. But if it was me, I'd be more worried about gettin' that egg off before it dries rock hard and wrecks yer paint."

True to his word, Officer Christy wrote the report while Jon paced back and forth beside his car and Caleb went to connect the garden hose. By the time the officer had gathered Jon's signature and reloaded himself into his patrol vehicle, Caleb had soaked the entire surface of the car and was filling a bucket with sudsy water for the second washing.

"Hey, grab a brush," he called over to where Jon was still standing, looking out after the patrol car.

"What?"

"I said get a brush. We've got to get this stuff off and see how bad the real damage is."

Obediently, Jon picked up a sponge and began to scrub away the crusted egg.

❧ ❧ ❧ ❧

A mental checklist pursued Esther even onto the airplane. The arrangements for someone else to fill in for her at work, the suitcases so hastily packed, the rental car that would need to be available in Omaha, the tickets in hand for the quick return trip Monday morning, and, haunting her, the thought that she had still not been able to get in touch with Neal.

Annie had been wonderful. She had spent the night at Esther's house, listening and comforting, and had made herself available for every errand her distraught friend had thought important while Esther would be gone. By morning, Esther's nerves had taken more than they seemed capable of bearing, and she could feel herself trembling as the plane lifted off the runway and headed into the clouds.

The drive south from Omaha seemed to take forever as she steered the car through Lincoln and then onto the smaller country roads which led to the valley where her small town was tucked away. Familiar road marks covered with a spring snow had become strange and unnatural to Esther in the five years since she'd been home. There were so many things that had changed: roads widened, buildings erected, and old landmarks torn down or altered. The closer Esther came to her home, the more startling the changes.

But the most difficult part of the drive, by far, was through Cold Mill. The ghosts of her memories seemed to beckon from every storefront and side street. Here was the place where she had been cornered by an angry dog, there was where Benny MacCloud had asked her to go steady, and just beyond that park bench was where she had fallen and broken her arm while roller-skating. Every memory seemed anxious to burst into Esther's mind at once—each dragging behind it all of the emotion the flashback had stirred.

From Main Street, Esther turned onto Elm, the street where she had grown up. The glorious elms that had once marked the street were all but gone, only three or four having escaped disease. Instead, a much less inspiring set of poplars had been planted to take their place, and they vainly struggled to mimic the grandeur of their predecessors.

Esther idled the car past new garages and empty front lawns that had once held brightly painted picket fences. Then, suddenly, she was in front of Andy's house. The many cars filling the road in front of it and lining the driveway made it difficult to determine if his house had changed. But the second-floor window at Andy's old room stared down at Esther, and she wiped away a thin trail of tears, knowing she should have been home long ago—she shouldn't have neglected their friendship. It was incredible to face the house and know that Andy was not there to greet her.

Then her car nosed its way past the last of the row of visitors' vehicles and her front yard came into view. Esther touched her brakes in order to survey it carefully. The trellis her father had so meticulously framed near the front door was gone. Esther felt the stab in the deepest part of her being. The grass was badly neglected and the porch in need of painting. Anger edged into the foreground of her heart. Even the bushes had been allowed to become overgrown and ugly.

Releasing the brake, Esther pulled away from her old home and continued down the street. Her mind was working furiously now; she was beating back the emotion she had so recently allowed to surface. She was pushing and pressing and prying all of the unwanted baggage she had carried for so long back into the furthest recesses of her mind. *I cannot feel those things now.* They were more than she was able to control. And in the end, the only emotion inside her strong enough to overcome her greatest efforts to contain it was her anger, which stubbornly poked itself out and provoked her with its very presence.

Esther drove away from Elm Street. She drove past the rows of familiar houses and turned the rental car toward the new subdevelopment whose tract houses were lined along each side of the narrow street. Here was dramatic contrast to her own street. Here were houses each the same size and shape as the two on either side. Here were stunted bushes and fenceless front yards.

Esther double-checked the address she had scribbled in her planner on the seat beside her, then cast a dubious eye down the row of mailboxes on her left. *Eleven forty-nine—eleven fifty-three—fifty-seven. There it is. Eleven sixty-one Cavanaugh Way.*

Esther pulled into the narrow driveway and nudged the car to a stop. Allowing herself only a brief moment to sit and survey the house, she climbed out onto the packed snow and trudged to the front stoop. The soft tones of the doorbell echoed inside and she turned her back to wait for a response. It was not long in coming.

The door flung open. "Esther!"

Turning again toward the door, Esther could feel her anger weaken. "Mom," she choked out, then buried herself in the woman's embrace.

# Nine

*Saturday, March 27*

Esther helped herself to another cup of coffee and poured some sweetener in. Her mother was busy beside her, compulsively mixing another batch of muffins to add to the several dozen she had already made for the grieving family. She and her mother had enjoyed sharing a kitchen once. Esther could remember the pleasure they had anticipated at offering her father a new dish they were sure he'd like. The recollection made her throat tighten.

"Where do you keep your spoons, Mom?"

"Over there. In the drawer beside the refrigerator."

Esther walked to it and drew out a spoon, eyeing the drawer suspiciously and surveying its contents. "Didn't you even keep the silverware?" Before all the words had passed her lips, Esther was sorry she had spoken them.

Glenna Branson's head jerked up from the muffins she was mixing, but she refused to look toward her daughter. "I still have them. They're in a box in the basement if you want them. I didn't feel like I needed silver for everyday use." There it was, the beginning of a discussion they had managed to avoid during their few telephone conversations. Esther could feel the dam of unspoken thoughts eroding between them.

"You could have had any of it if you'd bothered to come home and help me pack." The words stung, perhaps more than intended.

"I couldn't, Mom. I told you that. It was too hard."

"Then why not the next summer, or the Christmas after that? Why haven't you come home since?"

Words were a struggle; conflicting emotions grappled to gain control. "Because I didn't have a home anymore." Tears were forming, disregarding Esther's attempts to avoid them. "Because you sold the house as soon as Daddy died and I didn't have a *home* to come back to." The emotional dam had broken. There was nothing left now but to be swept along by its turbulent forces.

"Two months, Esther." Her mother was shaking, waving a hand toward Esther. "Two months I sat in that house, crying and aching to have him back. Two months I slept in the bed where he should have been—and walked past your door, thinking how good it would be to hear your voice. How dare you blame me for selling the house when it hurt me too badly to stay! You were the one who said it hurt you too much to even come home! You, of all people, should have understood."

"I came home." Esther's heart had heard only the accusation. "I came back from college the minute I heard that Daddy was gone. I drove through the night to get here, and then I took care of everything. Who made the funeral arrangements, Mom? Not you—you were holed up in your bedroom alone. Who had to face all the people? With their flowers and cards and—"Esther threw out a hand toward the mixing bowl—"and their stupid muffins! Who made it easier for me, Mom? Who comforted me and let me have my chance to cry?"

"He was my husband," Glenna gasped through her increasing tears.

"He was my daddy!" Esther screamed and retreated to

the guest bedroom where she slammed the door. Collapsing onto the bed, Esther clutched a pillow and rocked back and forth, allowing herself a rare moment of unrestrained grief. She wept for the father she had lost just after leaving home. She wept for the mother whose love she was throwing away with both hands. And, in great waves of sorrow, she was finally allowing herself to weep at the loss of her dearest childhood friend. Together, the griefs tumbled over one another in torment.

The afternoon sun was shining fully into the room when Esther finally began to gather herself. She wasn't sure if she had slept at all, or whether her eyes refused to focus because of her crying. At any rate, it would be close to the time of the funeral service, and Esther forced herself to get up and walk back to the kitchen. It was quiet and empty. The muffin batter had been abandoned and was now crusted over—the spoon almost buried where it had slipped down the inside of the bowl.

"It's almost time to go." Esther jumped at the words from behind her.

Glenna had already dressed for the funeral. Her shoes dangling from one hand, she had padded up behind Esther quietly. Now they surveyed one another through familiar emotional veils.

"I should get dressed, too."

"We need to leave in about half an hour."

Esther walked back to the bedroom and closed the door, relieved to be alone again. Slipping on a black dress that Annie had packed for her, she surveyed herself in the mirror. The dress was an unadorned, straightforward style that would be appropriate for a funeral, but Esther knew she would never be able to wear it again. With little interest, she dabbed makeup around her puffy eyes, then turned her back on her own reflection.

It was Esther who drove them to the church. Falling in

line behind the other mourners who were stamping snow from their shoes and silently entering the church to take a seat in front of the closed coffin, Esther was stoic again. Deliberately, Esther chose a pew as far as she could from the one she had been seated in during her father's funeral.

The congregation's new pastor took his place behind the podium and began the service with a prayer. Then Esther listened to the special music and the tributes that were given. *Muriel is now a teenager*, she noted, *and the older sisters are married.* Andy had died an uncle to several children, scattered along the back row of the sanctuary, too young to grasp what was going on and carefully watched over by other family members.

The only time during the service that Esther had been close to losing composure was when Mrs. Gray was escorted by her husband on her way out to the waiting limousine for the ride to the cemetery. Esther was able to feel the grief etched into the lines of her face. But she could see something else there, too. A strength. A peace. It seemed to burn like a laser into Esther's own inner turmoil.

After the short graveside ceremony, she forced herself to approach Mrs. Gray. She was instantly recognized. "Esther," the woman reached out warmly. "It was so kind of you to come. It means so very much to see you here. Oh, you're even more beautiful now."

Esther could not respond. She reached out in return and hugged the older woman.

"Please stop by the house when you can. I'd like a chance to talk with you and see how you're doing. We've missed you so."

*Missed me so? Means so very much to see me? Would like to talk?* Esther smiled dumbly in response and retreated to her car. How could Mrs. Gray appear so composed? How was it she could even speak at such a time? Where had she found the strength to face her only son's funeral without collapsing?

The drive back to her mother's house was as quiet as the drive to the church had been. In silence they ate reheated stew for supper and, with as little conversation as they could manage, spent the evening together until it was late enough to excuse themselves and go to their own beds.

In the morning, Esther dressed and ate breakfast alone. She was aware her mother had long since stopped attending church, but that seemed to be all the more reason that Esther should. Her choice between spending another few hours in silence at the house or taking the opportunity to get away for a while was an easy one to make. There had not even been a question raised as to where Esther was going. Apparently, her presence would not be missed.

Back inside her home church, Esther was relieved to see no signs of the funeral service that had taken place there the day before. Even the flowers had been removed, presumably taken back to the Grays' house for display. Esther shuddered. The last thing she had wanted when her father died was to be near all those gaudy vases of dying flowers.

As soon as the last phrase of the last song was sung, Esther struck out for the door. The old building held no place of refuge for her after all, and she wanted to avoid coming face-to-face with the few familiar people who remained there.

For some time, Esther drove around her old town, marking the changes in her mind and resenting them with all her heart. *Why can't I go back to the time before I left for college?* There had been so much good around her then. The town had been comfortable and stable. Her world had been full and pleasurable. There had been no skeletons to tuck away in the closets of her mind.

And then it came to her. There was one anchor left from that world. *Granddad's home.* It had been years since Esther had visited him in his home. There had been Christmases together at her aunt's house, but she hadn't been back to Granddad's house for so very long. Maybe, just maybe, seeing his old house would bring her the comfort she was seeking. And maybe he could offer some consoling words to her aching heart.

The house was not in Cold Mill. It was in a nearby county in an even smaller town about thirty miles away. Esther drove to it, feeling hopeful and frightened at the same time. What else might have changed?

But Granddad's house was just the same. The same gray siding. The same cracked cement step. The same fish-shaped plaque reading "Morris and Camilla Branson" hanging beside the white trim of the front door, even though he had lost Grandma so many years before. Esther held her breath while she waited for an answer to her knock.

"Esther. I hoped you would come to visit." He was home. And it was just as she remembered. Immediately he reached out to embrace her. Even though he was nearly eighty, there was a strength and authority that Granddad projected, as well as the tenderness that he had always displayed. It may have had much to do with his height or the deep tones of his voice, but Esther had always felt as if there were nothing too difficult for him. *Coming to see him was the right choice.*

"Come in, come in." He helped her out of her coat, then ushered her into his living room, chatting as he did. Esther was pleased again to note how little he had changed. His hair was still thick and full, brushed back on all sides as it had always been, though it had for many years been entirely gray. Even his clothing seemed to be the same as when she had last seen him. The brown leather shoes, the pleated dress slacks, the striped collared shirt, though he was not wearing the usual tie.

Leaning deep into the familiar chesterfield and tucking her feet under her, Esther allowed herself to relax. For a long time, she shared bits and pieces with her grandfather of what she was doing in Atlanta. Sitting in his easy chair and looking across at Esther, he listened quietly, asking all of the right questions. "I hope to get a chance to meet this Neal of yours. You've always made him sound like such a good man. I'm sure I'd love him, too."

Esther nodded silently, fidgeting with her engagement ring unconsciously.

"And how is your mother?" her grandfather went on.

Esther struggled for the right words. "She's all right, I guess. We . . . um . . . I'm afraid we had a little fight."

"Good."

Esther frowned at his answer. "Excuse me?"

"I said, 'good.' You two have not been the same since Perry passed on. Every time you're together I can see a wall between you, and it's time you faced each other and your feelings."

"What do you mean?"

"Esther, I'm your granddad. I don't have time, patience, or tact enough to keep my thoughts to myself. Dear, dear child. She's your mother."

Esther could not meet his gaze.

"She loves you. And you love her, too. Don't let this trouble between you keep you apart. Perry would have been ashamed to know the anger between you had lasted this long."

Esther wanted to tell him, to share with him all of her reasons for being hurt. She told herself she wasn't sure whether or not it was fair to drag him into her affairs. But in the end he coaxed all of the emotions out of her.

With tumbling words, Esther poured out her heart to the aging man. His softened hands patted hers and his gentle coaxing brought out truth that Esther had not fully faced, even in her own thoughts. She was angry at her mother for not being stronger when her father had died. And she was angry that Glenna had given up on the house so quickly instead of staying in it to keep his memory alive. She was angry that her bedroom would never be hers again, that the bookshelves her father had built for her now held someone else's trophies and treasures. She was angry that all her special nooks and crannies had become some other child's places of fantasy, and that the yard where her daddy had taught her to play catch had been claimed by someone else's children. With tears streaming down her cheeks, Esther choked out that she could barely live with the idea that the grave of her dog had been sold away—the dog her father had given her for her eighth birthday, the dog they had trained and loved and spoiled. And when she thought of all of her father's workmanship, where she had handed him nails or shined the flashlight on just the right spot—that all he had carefully improved in the oversized home had been lost to them, Esther could hardly speak. And she could not even look up as she verbalized the final nagging thought. If she had been willing to come home instead of pursuing her career, could she have saved the family's home?

Who was she really angry at? What specifically had her mother done wrong? She couldn't put it into words. But as they talked it seemed that she felt her mother had sold the home out of spite that Esther had not come home to stay—that it had been done expressly to punish Esther.

Was there any evidence her suspicions were valid? No, there was none. What if it really was her mother's pain, and not her mother's resentment, that had caused her to sell the house? What if her own anger had been misdirected?

So then was it really Esther's fault for leaving? For not dropping out of college, or at least, for moving to Minnesota instead of coming home? What should she have done differently? Should she have given up her dreams in order to live close to her mother and fill her need for companionship? Was it realistic to expect that from herself?

Granddad listened. In his skillful way, he answered Esther's questions by rephrasing them and giving them back to

Esther to answer. Issue by issue, the layers of painful thoughts were stripped away.

"She loves you, Esther. She always loved you—pampered you and nurtured you. There wasn't a need or a wish that your mother didn't try to meet for you. You were loved totally and unconditionally by both of your parents."

"Then why? Why are we so angry and closed to each other now?"

"I've seen it before. Death can be a great wedge that drives itself between people and chokes out all other shared experiences. It doesn't need to be that way, but that is often what it becomes."

"But why, Granddad? Why didn't it bring us closer? Can't a death do that, too?" Esther thought about the Gray family and the closeness exhibited at Andy's funeral.

"Oh, dear child. It can. But only when we are able to take our eyes off of what death is to us and see it from God's perspective."

"What do you mean?"

Granddad sighed and looked away sadly. "I failed my family, Esther. For some reason, I wasn't able to pass my faith on to your father. He accepted religion—going to church and striving to be upright. But I wasn't able to make him understand that life is eternal, and that everything we see around us is only a small part—an appetizer—for what we will have in heaven. If I had been able to teach him that, perhaps he could have made you understand, too. Perhaps your mother could have let him go. Perhaps there need not have been a wedge, because there would have been hope."

"But he did teach me, Granddad. Daddy was very religious. It was very important to him."

Another sigh. "That is true of so many. They want to *say and do* what seems right to the people around them. But sometimes it isn't because they want to please God; it's because they want to appear good to their fellowman. That isn't what God wants from us at all. I knew that. I tried to teach it to my son, but I'm not sure I succeeded."

"Granddad! You did succeed. Daddy was good—truly good, through and through. How can you think he didn't love God? What father could look at my dad and not be proud and grateful for who he was and what kind of life he lived?"

"Careful, child. Go carefully, now. I didn't say I wasn't proud of your father. Perry was one of the finest men I have ever known. And I didn't say he wasn't a Christian. No one can say that about another person. We can only find that answer for ourselves. But I'm old, Esther, and I've had so much time to look back at my life. I do realize that I was not the father I should have been. I should have spent much more time teaching my family to seek God instead of traveling so often and writing so much in an attempt to be successful. Perhaps I didn't truly discover God for myself until I had already raised your father and sent him off into the world."

Esther struggled in her mind with all of the implications. *If going to church isn't the way to please God, if truly seeking God with one's heart is required, what does that say about my own faith?* "Then, how can people ever know if they've found God and they're pleasing God with their life?"

"Are you asking on your father's behalf or on your own?"

"Both—I guess."

"We can't speak for Perry. Only God can know his heart—though I do have peace when I think of him. I remember some of the things he said to me in his last years, and I feel peace. As for you, I can't speak for you, either. You must answer that for yourself."

Esther turned her face to the floor. "I don't feel like God is very close to me. I'd like to. I do think about it sometimes—and I'd really like to know for sure."

"Oh, Esther. You can! Whenever you're ready, you can talk to God and just tell Him that you want Him to be a part of your life—that you want Him to be near you in everything you do."

"I don't pray very well." Esther had cried so much in the last two days, she was surprised there were any tears left to spill—but they were forming in her eyes just the same. "I always feel like I'm saying the wrong things."

"There are no wrong things to pray if your heart is speaking to God, child. Just be honest and tell God how you're truly feeling." Granddad's eyes were moist with tears, too, but his smile was deep and full. "Are there questions I can help you answer?"

"Well, I prayed 'the prayer' when I was young, but I've always doubted if it worked. I prayed with my Sunday school teacher, Mrs. Garrison, who I just loved and wanted so badly to please. That's why I could never believe that anything changed. I was so sure that my reasons were wrong and that God wouldn't want anything to do with me."

"And you understand why it is that your heart feels far from God? You understand that sin is the barrier between you and the most holy Being in our universe—you know that it is the sin in your heart that has kept you from turning to God all this time?"

Esther's face leaned into her hands. "I know. I know that I'm selfish. Just look how I've treated my own mother."

"What do you want to change, dear?"

"I want to *know* that when I pray, I'm being heard. I want to know that God is more than just a vague idea hovering out there somewhere. I want to know what He's like and understand all the reasons that He's done what He has. I want to be sure I'm doing this for the right reasons and that I'm pleasing God." Esther stopped for a moment to let her words sink into her own consciousness. "Granddad, could I? Could I really know that my life was pleasing God?"

"Yes. Yes, child, you could know."

"I want that." Her lip was trembling. "I want to be sure."

Granddad reached across to place his hand on Esther's knee. First he prayed on Esther's behalf, that God would make her understand what was needed for her life to be changed. Then Esther stumbled over a few words of a prayer that seemed to be drawn from the very core of her being. "I've always known about you," she whispered. "I just have never really known you for myself. But I want to. . . ."

For some time they prayed together. Esther, in the presence of her grandfather, confessed the ways she knew she had been wrong in her life. It was as if it had suddenly been brought into focus and she could see herself for the first time as God had seen her. And that vision caused her to realize she could not earn her way into God's presence by her attempts to live uprightly. Her own effort would *never* be enough. There was remorse; there was even shame, but as Esther's heart was laid bare, there was an overwhelming knowledge that she was finally making things right and gaining what she had wanted for so long.

And she became sure of the Jesus of her childhood—God's Son, the King of Kings, who had been born in a manger, who had lived a life of love and service to all of the people who had crowded around Him, who had allowed himself to be crucified, even though He could have so easily stopped His executioners, and who had come back to life and defeated death—Esther knew now the full impact of the stories she had been taught. It had all been for her, and for people just like her. Jesus had lived and died so that she could face a perfect God and not be condemned by the ugliness of her own heart—because that heart had been made clean and new again.

When at last they had poured out all of the things they had wanted to say in prayer, Esther sat back and sheepishly looked around, a tentative smile flickering across her face.

There had been no light from heaven, no unnatural sounds or sensations, but Esther was different. She knew in her heart that she had been changed. And for that, she was very grateful. With puffy eyes and a broad smile, Esther reached out to hug her granddad and could not restrain the laughter welling up inside her.

# Ten

*Sunday, March 28*

The door closed stiffly behind Esther when she walked through her mother's living room and into the kitchen. Evidently Glenna had been working there earlier: a pot of potato soup simmered on a back burner and a fresh salad waited in a bowl beside the sink. Esther continued down the hallway and called softly.

"I'm in the laundry room." The answering voice was flat and tired.

"Hi. I'm home." Her awkwardness was overwhelming. "I visited Granddad."

For a moment, Glenna raised her eyes to Esther's face and then went back to hanging shirts.

*Please, Lord. If the commitment I've just made is real, then help me know what to say to Mom.*

"We had a long talk." Still no response. "I learned a lot, Mom. About myself, and about Daddy dying, and about . . . well . . . about why I was so angry." Glenna's shoulders rose defensively, but Esther continued. "I need to tell you how sorry I am. I don't know if you can forgive me now, but I want you to know that I never, never meant to hurt you. And that I'm so sorry for what I said."

The face came up, the eyes misted. Esther could see her

uncertainty. And suddenly Esther realized how much pain her eyes held—how difficult the loss had been for her mother. The anguish that drove her to sell the old house became so clear. *How could I have been so blind?*

"I don't want you to be alone, Mom. I want us to be friends."

"Oh, Esther." Glenna was crying again. "I'm sorry for what I said, too. I can hardly believe I spoke to you that way. I don't know why I did. Those weren't the things I meant to say. All afternoon I agonized about what a horrible mother I am. But it's as if I can't help it. I just get so angry about what my life has become. I sit here alone day after day feeling empty and abandoned. I get mad at you for not calling—and I still even get angry at your father for leaving me. I know that doesn't make any sense. I tell myself over and over that it doesn't make any sense. I know it wasn't his fault, but sometimes I feel so lonely I just wish I could die."

Words wouldn't even form for Esther. For some time they let the tears fall, hugging each other and trying to soothe the wounds unwittingly inflicted. At last, they both stepped back, uncertain as to what to do next.

"Are you hungry?" Glenna asked. Together they headed to the kitchen for soup, and a chance to share heartfelt conversation, so long overdue.

Esther could feel their relationship slowly rebuilding. It would not be as it had once been. Her childhood picture of Glenna Branson was gone: neither of them was the same person now. But they could begin again. They could learn to understand and accept each other for who they were now. And Esther was so grateful that her mother wanted to restore the relationship, too.

As evening fell, Esther drove to the Grays' home. It had not been an offhanded remark that Mrs. Gray would like to see Esther. She was certain the dear neighbor would have been very much offended had she returned home without stopping in for a short visit.

Muriel answered the door to Esther's knock. Since Muriel had been too young to remember her when Esther left for college, she introduced herself and asked if it was a good time to visit. Without hesitation, Muriel invited her in and showed her to the family room, where friends and family members still in town were gathered.

During the next couple of hours, Esther sat with Andy's family, sharing the aftermath of their grief. Having spent much of their first wave of tears, they remained together to share comfort, to acknowledge that the loss had been great, and to avoid having to bear it alone. Esther was glad she had come.

Someday, in the not-too-distant future, she would write to Mrs. Gray about how the weekend had brought a great change in her life—but not now. The kindly neighbor had a right to her grief, uninterrupted by what was happening in Esther's life.

During the rest of the evening and late into the night, Esther chatted with her mother, catching up on all of the things they would have shared with each other through the recent years had they been able. Esther also discusses with her mother her conversation with Granddad and the prayer they had said together, though she was almost certain she had not been fully understood. Perhaps her mother would need time to grasp the significance.

Once Glenna had gone to bed, Esther returned to her own room and repacked her suitcases for the next morning. So many thoughts still echoed in her mind, and the late hour gave Esther the reflection she needed to bring some measure of closure to the amazing chain of events that day.

Monday morning came far too early. Esther had begun to grow accustomed to her late nights, but her early mornings had faded into late risings. Now her body protested, disturbed again from its routine.

At the door of her mother's home, suitcases resting on the step beside her, Esther turned. "I'm going to miss you, Mom," she whispered.

"I'm so glad you came, and that we talked. It's much easier to let you go back to Atlanta now that I don't feel like you're anxious to leave."

Esther smiled meaningfully. "But it makes it harder to go."

"Then we'll have to call each other more often."

"I know we will. I love you, Mom."

"I love you, too."

On the way out of town, Esther pulled her car to a stop in front of the cemetery and surveyed the area where Andy's freshly dug grave rose above the blanket of white snow on the ground.

So little of the weekend had been spent thinking about Andy. Esther was almost ashamed to look out at his grave. But she needed to acknowledge his death in some way, though she wasn't even sure what she hoped to accomplish by stopping at the cemetery on her way out of town.

She whispered aloud, "God, I know he's with you now. If he can see me, if he knows at all what's going on back here without him—or if he cares at all about that right now—please tell him, for me, that I'm going to miss him. Really, truly miss him. I'll never have another friend like Andy. Somehow, he's part of me—part of who I am. But if he knows what happened this weekend—if he's watching me—I know that Andy will be glad to hear he still had a lot to do with bringing me back to face my past. He always tried to tell me there was something I was missing. I know he would be glad to know I've finally found it." A single tear slid down

Esther's cheek. "I wish I could just talk to him one more time . . . to tell him I finally understand."

Then Esther forced herself to drive away, leaving behind her hometown but taking with her new courage and hope.

# Eleven

*Monday, March 29*

Esther arrived in Atlanta with just enough time to catch a taxi back to her house and dress for work before she needed to leave again—stopping only to listen to her telephone messages, most of them from Neal. His voice held increasing frustration with each message. Esther hoped he wouldn't be angry once he had heard her explanation.

Finally, she pulled into the parking lot minutes before she was due in the afternoon editorial meeting, breathing a sigh of relief that she hadn't been delayed by traffic. The remaining time until the six o'clock broadcast was hardly more than a blur.

As much as Esther would have liked to, she had not been able to find time to talk with Annie during the late afternoon. An urgent need for video footage from several months back had Annie searching through tapes of previous shows. Someone had failed to document which show a live interview had taken place on, and since it had been a last-minute addition, it was not included in the script for the night. Watt was spewing expletives to everyone around him about failing to document work. Esther chose to avoid the area.

In some ways, Esther felt that she was walking through a dream. *Was there really a change in my heart yesterday?* She'd hardly even had time to wonder until she sat down to have her hair done and her makeup applied before going on set. As she relaxed against the padded chair and closed her eyes while the beautician worked, Esther tried to sort through what changes she expected.

Of course, there had been a drastic improvement in her relationship with her mother. There was no denying that. But how many other areas of her life would the prayer affect? And how would she ever know that what she had experienced was genuine? She had never doubted God was real, and she had always tried to live by the moral code she knew came from the Bible. But was there still more that needed to change?

And there was no denying that another question loomed in the shadows of her unformed thoughts. Would a short prayer and an afternoon of honesty and reparation of old wounds affect her here, so far away from Granddad and her mother? What if her prayer had not really changed her at all? What if she had experienced only a time of emotional energy? Surely there had to be more to this accepting of God into her life than what she had already done. *But what?*

Long before she was ready, Esther was launched into the broadcasting session. She smiled, she informed, she asked questions; but the words seemed to come from someone else. If only she could stop the world for just a little while and try to catch her breath.

Tuesday morning dawned clear and warm. Esther stretched across the printed rosebuds on the soft cotton sheets, feeling lazy in the rays of sunlight that streamed through the bedroom window and painted a splash of warmth and brightness on the comforter. She was home. It was a wonderful feeling to wake up, rested and peaceful, in her own bedroom. For only a moment or two, she allowed herself the luxury of closing her eyes again and drifting back into sleep. Then her mind snapped back to all of the things that needed to be accomplished during the morning because of her absence. The lazy feeling disappeared like a mist and Esther rose dutifully to shower and begin the day. No, the world did not stop, so she mustn't, either. She must just try to keep up.

All morning Esther ran the errands she had missed doing over the weekend. Grocery shopping, dropping off dry cleaning, vacuuming her car, and stopping by to have her nails done were chores she usually accomplished on Saturday, as well as the inevitable list of items postponed during the week.

Once those were done, it was time to rush off to work again, ready to face another day of peering into the newsworthy elements of other people's lives—having barely enough time to attend to her own.

First on her agenda was tracking down as much information on the elusive Jon Shepherd as possible. Using the phone, she was able to pinpoint his hometown in Wisconsin and his second job—an inner-city education and outreach center that had been featured a year ago in the local paper. Her interest piqued, Esther decided her best chance to land a possible interview with Mr. Shepherd would be to learn as much as she could about the youth center, and perhaps appeal to him as a fellow Midwesterner. *But not by contacting him directly*, Esther decided. Everyone would be trying that. She would have to think of a better way.

She still hadn't been able to get in touch with Neal, and she was growing more anxious about it as the day crawled by. There was so much she needed to tell him, and she was uncertain as to how he would react.

Once again, the sense of a change in her outlook followed Esther. It was as if she were adjusting to a new set of prescription glasses—seeing her environment in a strange and startling new way. She found herself watching people far more closely, with more than a passing interest. Did they know she was concealing a private joy and satisfaction today? Should she try to tell someone? Even Annie would be difficult to face with the explanation. Would she understand?

It was late in the day by the time Esther finally reached Neal. His business trip had been extended, and he was frantic with worry that he hadn't been able to contact her.

"I can only talk a minute. I'm due in a meeting, but I wanted to try to reach you one more time."

"What is going on? Since when do you leave town and fly around the country without talking to me first? Did you forget all about me?"

"Of course not, Neal. I tried several times to call you. I wish we had more time to talk now. It was such a tough weekend for me, with Andy's funeral and seeing Mom. I stayed at her house—drove right past our old home and stayed in the little house she had built after Daddy died." Esther let her words hang unanswered in the air. "We had a terrible fight that first morning. It was awful. And then with the funeral and all, I'm just exhausted. Look, I'd really like to be able to tell you everything in person. Do you think you could meet me for dinner when I get off work?"

"Esther, I had a long weekend, too. You don't get off until well after eleven-thirty. I'd really rather not meet you tonight. I just wish you would have tried harder to reach me this weekend."

His tone was making Esther feel defensive. Surely, there must be more to his reaction than what he was admitting to. It was so unlike Neal to be short with her. "I tried to reach you several times. Look, I really can't talk now. Gabe is waving me over. I could meet you in the morning, but I know you don't like to start work late. Couldn't we just take a little time to talk tonight? At El Presidente, about twelve?"

Neal muttered an unintelligible comment, then conceded to meet her at the restaurant.

*That didn't go well*, she thought. Esther and Neal so

rarely exchanged cross words. She was hoping his mood would improve by the time they met for supper. Perhaps the weekend conference had not gone well for him.

Esther's first steps toward the table where Neal was waiting for her revealed that his frustration had not weakened. He was visibly annoyed and short-tempered. His posture was slumped, something very rare for Neal, and his fingers curled and uncurled the cloth napkin while he waited for their order to be taken.

Perhaps tonight was not the time to approach him with all she wanted to share about her weekend. "How was the conference, Neal?" Esther reached out to place her hand over his.

"Why didn't you have me paged?" His brow was furrowed. She was surprised that he had not even acknowledged her question. Apparently, he had used the afternoon to analyze why their failure to communicate had been her fault.

"I didn't know which conference center your meeting was being held at. You mentioned Fort Worth, but I never got the name of the building." Esther forced her voice to be gentle and controlled. She hated difficult discussions in public places, but she could feel herself growing angry. During such a difficult situation for her, he seemed to be expecting her to spend time tracking him down. Surely, he didn't understand what he was asking. "And did you want me to page you during the funeral, or while I was fighting with Mom?" Immediately Esther regretted the words. She hadn't intended to sound quite that short in her response.

She could tell that Neal was trying to keep his own emotions under control. "Do you have any idea how worried I was?"

Perhaps that was a clue. Neal was reacting strongly because of his concern for her safety. "I'm sorry, Neal. I never meant for you to worry. And I did leave three messages on your voice mail. I couldn't think of anything else to do. Really, it was the situation—not what either of us did or didn't do—that was unfortunate."

"So that's it?" She hadn't made the least impression. "You fly out of town without so much as talking to me first and it's not your fault because I didn't listen to my voice mail? What about our commitment to each other? And what about your career, Esther? Did you stop to think how it looked to them that you had to find a replacement to tape the Monday daytime news breaks? You've only been an anchor for five short weeks. Don't you think that makes you look like a bad choice for the job?"

Esther stared in disbelief. That she had been to a funeral in her hometown and had suffered through a major family confrontation did not seem to interest Neal in the least. Somehow, he was implying that she had neglected her duties at work. "No one said it was a problem for Steve to fill in for me. It's not unusual for this sort of thing to happen. I'm sure I'll get a chance to return the favor for him. He as much as said so on Friday."

"What people say and what they're thinking are just never the same in business. Haven't you learned that yet? For all you know they're looking around again and making note of who might be able to replace you if you don't work out."

"That's ridiculous." Esther picked up her water glass and took a long sip, hoping he would change the subject.

"Well, Watt Shreve is not quite convinced."

Esther froze. *What did Neal just say?* "You talked to Watt? You *know* him?"

"I didn't say that." But Esther was almost certain she had seen Neal falter before answering.

"What *did* you say, then?"

"You were the one who said he went out on a limb to get you this job. He's bound to be worried that you're not going to work out. You've got to be dependable. Is there anything ridiculous about that, Esther?"

Neal's words had been whispered fiercely. Heads were starting to turn toward their table. The last thing Esther wanted was to make a scene. The woman at the next table was leaning their way, obviously listening for Esther's response to Neal. No matter how upset she was, Esther was determined not to put on a show for anyone in the dining room. Neal was too angry to know what he was saying. She would wait to discuss this further until he was ready to see things clearly. "We need to talk about this, but I don't want to do it here. I'm going to go freshen up, Neal. Go ahead and order for me."

Immediately, Neal's face hardened. He picked up his menu and sank down behind it. Esther rose quietly, slipped out of the room and into the hallway. When she returned, neither one mentioned the argument again that night.

❧ ❧ ❧ ❧

When Jon arrived home from the youth center the following evening, he flicked on the answering machine to check his messages. A man named Dr. Lloyd Finley, who worked at the science institute to which Jon had written asking for assistance, had left his phone number and said he would like to talk with Jon about his letter.

The wait until the following day to return the call was tough for Jon. He barely slept as the anticipation weighed heavily on him. Finally, at exactly 9:01, Jon dialed the number.

"Good morning, Genesis Research Association, may I help you?"

"Yes, my name is Jon Shepherd. I'm returning a call to Dr. Lloyd Finley."

"Just a moment please." There was a click and then music while Jon waited.

Jon turned to sit against the desk, then remembered that he ought to be ready to jot down some notes. Quickly shuffling through papers on the desk, he stumbled across a pencil. His notebook was lying out of reach on the dining room table, so he'd have to write on whatever was handy. Too late, he remembered he had written out a list of questions, but those were also in his notebook.

"Good morning, Lloyd Finley's office."

"Yes, I'm returning a call to Dr. Finley. My name is Jon Shepherd."

"Can you hold?"

"Yes, ma'am."

He was not kept waiting long.

"Mr. Shepherd, good morning. I'm glad you returned my call."

"Please, call me Jon. And I appreciate your interest in my letter, Dr. Finley. I was impressed with your contribution to a book I've recently read, and I've been anxious to talk to someone about my situation."

"Good, good. I hope we can give you the help you want. Could you give me a little more information about how far your case has progressed?"

"Well, I'm not actually in court. It could be that I'm panicking for no good reason, but there's a small part of me that would like to see this issue get some exposure—as long as I'm prepared to give a good representation of the facts. Why should thousands of students who don't believe in evolution need to be told in school it's the only scientifically sound answer? That's not freedom of religion, that's indoctrination." Jon hadn't intended to launch into such an intense argument. He could tell he was too uptight, too strained by lack of sleep—and lack of daily employment. He tried to rein in his emotions.

"Can I ask you, Jon, what exactly did you teach that day? What was the situation briefly?"

Once again, Jon tried to describe carefully what he had said and how the students had responded. It wasn't easy to repeat the story, and Jon fought the urge to feel defensive about what he had said and done.

"Do you feel you were pressuring the students to believe you?"

"Dr. Finley, at that point, I didn't even know what *I* believed. And now that I've been reading up on the subject, I still can't say I have anything more than some theories. To me, the central issue is the need for less autonomy in public school education—to allow for a belief about origins other than that we descended from apes. Sure, it's science class, but there are scientists—even truly great ones—who have no trouble reconciling their religious views with their scientific observations. Shouldn't we, as teachers, be allowed to offer that information to the students, too—as long as it meshes with solid scientific principles? And it is wrong, morally deficient, and scientifically in error to say that evolution has been accepted as fact by the entire scientific community. There are just too many holes in the theory, even though ardent evolutionists have tried for decades to patch them all as quickly as they've been exposed." He stopped short, a little embarrassed. "But then, I guess I don't need to tell *you* that, do I?" Once again, Jon tried to back away from his intense emotions.

"You're quite an articulate man, Jon. That will serve you well."

"Thank you, sir." That was not the response Jon had expected. Suddenly, he felt a little sheepish.

"So you're interested in having your say, are you? I'm glad to hear it. You need to be aware that you will probably lose at your hearing and that you may well be taken to court to be removed from your teaching position. I see this as a potentially precedent-setting case. The issue has been building over the last decade in school systems all across the U.S., and we've expected this to come out at one time or another. How do you feel about that?"

Jon drew a breath and answered as honestly as he could. "I'm not ready now. But if I were, I think I would actually enjoy the chance."

"You mentioned in your letter that you're a Christian. That your parents were missionaries. Have you prayed about this?"

"Every day, sir."

"Are you a married man? Do you have a wife or kids?"

Jon hadn't expected this type of question. "No, I'm single. Why do you ask?"

"I don't know if we'd be in favor of putting a man with a family through what may be involved in this case. And I'm glad to hear that you'd consider going to trial, but I want to say up front that we won't press you in any direction if you do decide otherwise. We'll still give you any help we can." Dr. Finley explained further. "Actually, your name and situation was mentioned by a member of our staff last week. We like to keep abreast of what's going on in the news as it relates to our research."

Jon was genuinely surprised that his story had reached all the way to the Colorado-based institute. "What we'd like to do now, Jon, is fly you out here. We'd like a chance to get to know you better and for you to understand who we are and what we are trying to accomplish with our research. We'd like to mail you a ticket for a visit next week. Would you be interested in that?"

Instinct pricked at Jon to be cautious. "I'd be happy to come, Dr. Finley. And next week would work out well for me, but I'd be more comfortable arranging for my own ticket."

"Fine. Fine. If that makes you feel better, I can respect

that. Just let us know what day you're coming and I'll meet you at the airport."

"I'll do that."

"Do you have any questions that I can answer for you today?"

Immediately Jon's mind scrambled through all the questions his studies had provoked, all written out in detail in his notebook. "Uh . . . everything's so interwoven in my mind. Maybe I should hold my questions until I'm there. I guess I'd like to ask, though, if this type of case has been tried anywhere else in the country before now?"

"Not to my knowledge. At least, not one with significant national exposure. Well," he corrected his answer as an afterthought, "I guess I should say there was a case back in the 1920s. But we lost. Let's see if we can turn the clock back a little, shall we? I'd like to start the next century with God allowed back into American schools."

"So would I." Jon took a deep breath. It could be that he and the doctor shared the same vision. "I'll be back in touch, then, when I have my flight information."

"Fine. I look forward to speaking with you again, Jon."

"Thank you, Dr. Finley." Jon dropped the receiver back into its place.

❧ ❧ ❧ ❧

Esther spent the following Friday morning with Annie at her duplex, talking about her last weekend in great detail. She purposely avoided any reference to her argument with Neal, knowing how Annie would react.

Esther was a little uncertain of how to explain the talk with her granddad. She wasn't sure that her friend, who had never been the least bit interested in spiritual matters, would realize the significance of her prayer. And, as she expected, Annie didn't understand.

"I'm glad for you, Esther. If that's what you want and it makes you happy, I'm glad."

"Thanks, Annie."

"So are you different? Is there anything you can't do now that you did before? I hope not, because you never really did much before! You're about the most perfect person I know."

"Oh, please. No, it's still the same Bible that I was raised to live by. I just have come to see that it's much more than a rule book. It's really hard to explain. I wish I could say all this in a way that would help you understand. But I'm still trying to understand it myself, really."

"Well, I mean what I said. If it makes you happy, I'm all for this new religious kick. But I just don't want to see you putting any more pressure on yourself to be Snow White or something."

Esther laughed. "That would pretty much make you a dwarf, wouldn't it? Guess I'll just call you Dopey or Sleepy or something."

Annie didn't skip a beat. "Well, nobody has ever accused me of being Bashful!"

It was a silly conversation, but they both needed to laugh. It made them feel as if their carefree college days weren't quite so far in the past.

Lying in her bed that night, Esther thought back over her week so far. For five days, she had walked through her own world feeling like a stranger. After her initial questions about how her weekend prayer would change her life, it had become apparent to her quickly. Each morning, she had taken her Bible off the shelf and begun reading. She hadn't been sure how to begin, but she was convinced it was important to start. And from the moment she began she had seen how every story and every psalm could speak to her heart. She found that—far from being a chore—reading the Bible had become a deeply personal experience.

But as far as praying was concerned, Esther still felt awkward. Having no one she could easily ask about what was proper to say or request, she felt she was fumbling around quite a bit. Often she found herself apologizing in her prayers for not paying better attention in church. She worried that she should have known more about praying after attending Sunday school for most of her life.

At work, she had increasingly felt as if every sensation had been magnified, amazed that the events of her weekend could make so much difference in how she viewed her life and the people around her. For one thing, she smiled much more. It was as if her heart were singing, released from its cage of worry and guilt. All of the *should have done*'s that had confined it had been relegated to her past and were no longer pulling her back into worrying about them.

During editorial meetings, Esther felt she had come alive. Where once she was timid about giving a dissenting opinion, now she had grown stronger and more willing to share. Were they being careful to tell both sides of each story? Were they being cautious about accusing statements made without sufficient evidence to back them up? She was trying not to sound like the group's watchdog, but she was also no longer content to take a seat on the sidelines. Somehow, though, she managed to ignore the looks of disgust that Watt shot at her from across the room.

Still, a dark shadow had been cast over her week because of her fight with Neal. Each conversation with him that week had been strained. In fact, as the week had progressed, he had seemed to become increasingly short with her. Try as she might, Esther could not put her finger on what was upsetting Neal. Perhaps it had little to do with her at all. Perhaps it was trouble at work. Funny, though, he had not seemed to be distressed like this before.

Saturday dawned bright and clear. Esther had leisurely

plans for the day. She had purchased several perennials to plant in the barren beds around her new house. A few hosta plants and some day lilies were all that she could manage yet, but she allowed herself the luxury of making great plans for what she would do someday.

She was expecting Neal to arrive for lunch. Maybe if he could see that she'd done a little work improving the house and if she cooked a special meal for him, his gloomy mood would fade and he'd be bearable again. Esther had tried all week to find the proper words to pray for her relationship with Neal. Somehow, it had seemed one of the most difficult prayers to stumble through. Something about her requests always sounded strangely hollow, even though she knew they were coming from the depths of her heart. Surely, God would want her relationship with her fiancé to be made right again.

Just as Esther had cleaned up from her gardening and had placed her meager tools back in their proper places, she caught the muffled sound of the telephone ringing inside the house. Hurrying to answer it, she winced that she hadn't even had time to wash the dirt off her hands yet.

"Hello?"

"Esther. It's Neal."

"Hi. I was just about ready to start lunch. Are you on your way?"

"No. Actually, there's a change of plans. I can't make it for lunch. I'll have to call you later."

It wasn't possible for Esther to keep the disappointment from her voice. "Why, Neal? Is everything all right?"

"Yeah. I just had a call from an associate. He wants to meet with me right away. I can't go into it now, but I can't make lunch."

"All right. Dinner, maybe?"

"Maybe. Bye."

"Good-bye, Neal." Esther set the phone back in its cradle and turned to wash her hands in the sink. Neal would not see the landscaping today.

❧ ❧ ❧ ❧

Jon had no trouble getting a flight for Colorado on the following Monday. With a little more than a week until the hearing, he was airborne and heading for what he hoped would be a very informative couple of days. He had deliberately not scheduled the return flight until Thursday so he could get in some spring skiing—assuming the weather cooperated. Everyone had urged him to take a little time away, so he had conceded. Looking out the window of the airplane as it started its descent, Jon was glad he had decided to stay the extra days. He had forgotten how beautiful the Rockies were.

Striding up the chilly ramp into the airport, Jon's mind returned to the real reason for his trip. He had brought all of his reading material with him, as well as his battered notebook filled with questions. Now, if he could just pick out Dr. Finley from the crowd waiting outside the door.

"Mr. Shepherd? Jon?"

"Yes," he answered the man standing in front of him, extending his hand toward him in a firm handshake.

"I'm Lloyd Finley. It's good to meet you."

"You too."

With little other conversation, they trudged across the entrance to the airport and out into the brisk mountain air.

"I hope you brought a good jacket, Jon. I'm sure Atlanta doesn't feel like Colorado this time of year."

"Atlanta doesn't feel like Colorado *any* time of year," Jon smiled. "But I really do prefer this to the heat."

Jon spent the next two days feeling as if he were back in school himself. The facility had been set up in an old college campus and was used by a variety of scientists for their research. Apparently, various organizations and churches across the country contributed to its funding, and there were also a wide variety of books and publications that netted income for the center. Jon had been given the freedom to venture from building to building, chatting with any of the researchers whom he could find. With wide eyes, he scribbled notes and asked questions of anyone willing to talk. Like a mental sponge he tried to absorb every bit of information he was seeing and hearing. Most thought provoking, though, were the conversations he had with other visitors to the institute. They offered no additional scientific insight, but he became more and more struck by their remarks.

"I admire you, Mr. Shepherd. Too many people are willing to sit back and do nothing while our children are systematically initiated into the new cult of secularism. This is no accident—what's happening in our schools. This is a conspiracy."

*If this is a conspiracy, then who is leading it?* Jon had to fight himself to keep from shooting back a remark about his never having received that memo. Instead, he smiled and excused himself from the conversation.

"I'm tired of hearing that parents aren't concerned about what is being taught in our schools. How can we think we are doing a good job with our kids if we don't know anything about what they are learning during the majority of their day? And not just the science and math—I mean the ethics and values being taught, too."

True, it had been Jon's experience that many parents were just grateful for not having to deal with their own kids during school hours. Not all of them, by any means, but far too many for Jon not to feel his heart fall just thinking about the kids he had known who would rather be in school than at home.

"What's happening to us? Society just keeps getting more and more depraved. This downhill plunge of morals gets worse and worse. I wish I could have chosen when to have lived. I would definitely have chosen to live in a time before immorality got so out of hand."

*And when would that have been?* Jon had almost reeled when he heard this comment. *Do you think the pioneers were sinless? Or the Founding Fathers? Or even the Pilgrims? Have you ever studied history at all? Or read the Bible? It's not the time we're born into. It's the human hearts that we're born with—the level of depravity we're each capable of just because we're people. None of us is immune to it—and certainly no civilization or era of history.*

Along with his notes, Jon realized the trip was providing discussions that were shaping his philosophy—not one that he would be parroting back, but one that was forming in his own mind as he listened to each comment directed his way.

Then Jon entered a laboratory where one old man worked alone, peering through a geological microscope, patiently examining a small rock sample.

"Excuse me," Jon said.

The scientist looked up from his table.

"My name is Jon Shepherd. I'm just looking around the institute. Do you mind if I come in and ask you some questions? That is, if I'm not interrupting something you can't leave for a minute?"

"Please come in, Mr. Shepherd. I am Dr. Schuller." Jon recognized the distinctly German accent.

"*Guten Tag*, Dr. Schuller. *Woher sind Sie?*"

"I am from Munich. You speak German very well. How is it that you do?"

"My parents were missionaries. I grew up just outside of Hamburg."

"I see. And how long were you there?"

"I was born in Germany. My family moved back to the U.S. when I was fifteen."

"Have you been back to visit again? It's very different there now."

"I'd *like* to visit again, but I haven't been able to."

"Nor have I. Not since 1987." There was genuine sorrow in his tone. Dr. Schuller turned back to his work and chipped more fragments from the stone. "Would you like to see what it is I am looking at?"

"Yes. Thank you." Jon stepped closer, not certain what it was he should be looking for. "What is it?"

"It's rock. Very special rock."

"Okay. It looks like a rock. What makes it special?"

"This rock I made."

"Excuse me?"

"This is very important rock, Mr. Shepherd. I am experimenting to see if rock does not take millennia to come to be—if, under the right conditions, sedimentary soils can become rock very quickly—in only centuries of time. So this rock is one I made. Not in centuries of time, of course. But using materials in various stages, you see."

Jon's mind leaped ahead to where he felt their conversation was leading. "So you're trying to prove that the earth is young, that the layers of strata were formed during the flood and became rock all at once."

"No."

"No?"

"I am attempting to prove nothing. It is the understanding that I am seeking."

Jon looked carefully at the old man's expression. "I don't think I follow."

"When we start with a scientific theory, Mr. Shepherd, we put our minds already in a box. This is, to me, not good science. Then I see only what I am wanting to see. How can I truly observe if already I think I know the answer?"

"Is that what you believe a lot of scientists do? They only look for what they want to find?"

"Some, yes. Some, no. Me, I try just to look. And decide after what it is that I am seeing."

Jon's puzzled expression betrayed his thoughts.

"You know the story of Galileo, do you not?"

Jon nodded.

"The church, it did not want to look through his telescope. It was afraid—afraid to see what it did not believe to be true. Afraid God would be proved to be wrong. Foolish, eh? We know that now."

Jon was familiar with Galileo. "They say your vision in hindsight is twenty-twenty. You know, the church absolved him a few years ago."

"I had heard they did."

Something about the scientist's candor nudged Jon to speak from his heart. "I'm not a scientist, Dr. Schuller. I'm just a schoolteacher. And I've heard a wider variety of theories about the creation issue here at your center than I had even read about before I came. How is it that you can all work together in one place? Aren't you working against one another? Negating one another's work?"

"I cannot speak for others. Only for myself. I am here because upon one premise we agree. I need no other. And that is this, that God will not be proved wrong. The Bible, it does not lie. Perhaps it means what we, yet, do not understand, but it does not lie. And the earth, it does not lie, either. What? Do we think that God is mocking us? That He made the rocks and stars to say that which is not true? Ach . . . we must not be afraid to look, Mr. Shepherd. God is still to be trusted. It is we who are confused."

Understanding welled up in Jon as he realized just how much truth the aged scientist had given him. The questions, the worries and concerns that he had felt about finding just the right theory, this was not the proper focus for his struggle. He realized he had been searching in the wrong direction.

"I will tell you one other thing about which I am thinking, Mr. Shepherd. If we, the Christians, are fighting one another about which theory is true, how can we be also the light on the hill that we are to be? How can we be the one Church that Jesus prayed for?"

"You're right, Dr. Schuller. You're so right."

Jon finished his two-day tour of the science complex and knew that he was taking away from it a great deal of scientific information and ideas. But mostly, he was grateful that he had spoken with the German doctor, who had helped him determine the focus of his fight.

❧ ❧ ❧ ❧

A cold, hard gaze followed Esther around the kitchen. She wasn't sure what had brought about the sullen change in Neal's demeanor, but try as she might to coax him to confide in her, she had gotten no additional insight. And, far from subsiding, it seemed that he was becoming more distracted—more brooding—as each day had passed.

"How about a movie? We can go out, or even watch the one I just rented. It's supposed to be pretty good."

There was no response. Neal turned to leaf through the newspaper instead, rolling his eyes as he did so. Esther stood, studying him. Anger began to bubble up inside of her. Suddenly, it was more than Esther could take. She had hoped to repair their relationship, while he'd avoided all real communication for over a week.

"You don't have any right to treat me like this. If I've done something wrong, then tell me."

Neal closed the newspaper and seemed to be contemplating his next move.

"I said I was sorry about the other weekend," Esther rushed on. "If I could do it over again, well, I would have found a way to get ahold of you if I . . . if I had to hire a private detective to find you. Is that what you want?"

"It's not about the weekend."

"Then what? You want to tell me, Neal. If you hadn't wanted to tell me you wouldn't be here right now."

Finally, she had pushed the button she was searching for. Neal burst out with, "Okay, I'll tell you. You blew it, Esther. You don't know the strings I had to pull to get you that co-anchor position. Yeah, I admit it. I was involved. And now that I've got you there you're on some kind of a power trip. You're in meetings trying to be the station's conscience or something. They don't need a conscience, Esther. It's business. All they need is for you to do what you were hired for—to read the news. That's it. They're going to pay you big bucks just to sit in a chair and read the news, and for some reason—which is way beyond me—that's not enough. What are you thinking?"

"*You* got me the promotion? How?"

"What does it matter?"

"It matters to me. How, Neal? What strings can you pull at the station?"

"All the right ones. That's my job, remember? I get people promoted."

"I never asked you to do it. I would never have asked for that."

"Yes, you did. That was the plan—and you knew it. Nobody's that naïve."

"How, Neal? Who do you know?" Esther's mind was spinning. Then suddenly she knew. "You know Watt. Watt Shreve, of course! How could I have missed it?"

"Yeah, and I'm supposed to believe that? That you didn't know. You knew, and you've been pushing him around ever since."

"What!"

"For over a week you've been dogging him. Every day he calls my office. Every day he complains about you—your attitude, your ideas, your holier-than-thou rebukes."

This time it was Esther who was speechless.

"He only keeps you because he owes me. But he doesn't owe me that much, Esther. He's going to turn on you. Don't be a fool."

"Get out." She was surprised to hear her own voice sounding so calm. It certainly didn't express how she was really feeling. "Whether you believe me or not doesn't matter. I didn't know anything about this. And I won't be held responsible for the situation you created for yourself. You need to leave. I want time to think."

She had his attention now. Neal's eyes were flashing, looking at her as if she had lost her mind. "You don't mean that." But his unrelenting gaze was proof that he was taking her seriously enough.

"I do."

"You'd better be sure." This time he spoke to her with a cruel tone to his words. There was a threat implied. Esther could feel it.

"I am sure."

"This is my house."

Immediately, Esther's mind was whirling. He hadn't said that. He hadn't meant it. What could she say to him? What could she do? Her breath was coming in short gasps now.

"If you want me to leave, I will. Just say the word, and I'll pack today."

They measured each other from across the room, watching to see how far each would go in his comments. Then Neal rose and slowly began walking toward Esther. She could see the veins in his neck bulging, could see the way his hands were clenched at his sides, could see his eyes squinting in an angry scowl. They were facing each other, standing so close she could hear his breath. Looking down at her upturned eyes, he appeared to be still undecided, but his anger was building inside him until the glare was blazing down upon Esther.

Finally, he spoke. "I'm leaving" was all he said, then he

turned his back to her and walked out into the garage where he had parked his car. She heard the engine roar and then fade down the street.

Relief flooded over Esther. For those few moments that had seemed to take a lifetime to pass, she knew she had truly been afraid of Neal.

Then, with a gasp of despair, she realized he might not be back. Tears flowed as she came face-to-face with the fact that she may have lost Neal forever.

# Twelve

*Friday, April 16*

At last, it was the morning of the hearing. Jon had felt for so long that this day couldn't come quickly enough, until it finally had. With fumbling hands he tried to concentrate on shaving without nicking himself, but his thoughts strayed over and over from what he was doing. Walking out of the bathroom and dabbing at the small cuts on his neck, he almost tripped over the dog.

"Go lay down, boy," he commanded, unaware of the unusual sharpness of his tone. Commodore obeyed submissively.

His notebook. It had to be around here somewhere. Just last night he had been—oh, there it was. Scooping it up, he packed it carefully inside his briefcase. "Cale, you coming?"

"Right behind you" came the answer.

This time the hearing room was a buzz of activity. Jon was surprised to recognize some of the parents seated in the back, and even a couple of his students. For him, that was slightly unnerving. Then the hum of conversation subsided as the line of school board members filed in and took their places at the head table. Once again, Jon sat facing Henley Brinkner. This time, though, there was no pretense of friendliness.

"Ladies and gentlemen, may we have order, please?"

The proceedings were uncomplicated. First, the issue was laid out as clearly as possible. Then Jon was asked a few simple questions about what he had specifically said during the class. Following this, several school board members were given the chance to make comments or ask for further information. Even this did not prove to be time-consuming.

After they had each had a chance to speak, the microphone was opened to Jon for his comments. This was his chance to defend the actions he had taken.

"First, I just want to say to all of you who came today that I've been teaching for eleven years, and I've never had the least bit of trouble before. I'm not here because I like controversy or because I try to create conflict. I'm just a regular run-of-the-mill teacher who inadvertently ended up in the middle of this issue. Looking back, I wish I had understood the importance of discussing this with Denny—that is, Mr. Trent—before presenting it in class. If I had one thing to do over again, it would have been that.

"But I honestly believe it wouldn't have changed the core issue." Jon turned to look out over the crowded room. "Ladies and gentlemen—parents and students—I'd like you to understand that I wasn't preaching and I wasn't promoting anything. It's so important that you see I was making every effort to highlight the words 'theory' and 'idea.' There were plenty of students who disagreed, and even many who laughed outright. I never discouraged them from disagreeing with me.

"But we're also all aware of the guaranteed freedoms that make America what it is. And I've got to say that I believe it's time to rethink whether or not we should be able to refer to God in the scope of public education. We've allowed all manner of other topics, much less palatable to most of the general public, to be mentioned in textbooks. In fact, we're applauding our schools for teaching tolerance and diversity. Those are the new buzz words.

"This tolerance needs to include tolerance of the belief in God. Why can't we say some people believe God created the world? Why can't we acknowledge that? Many of my students believe it. Why should they have to suffer through lessons that deny God's very existence?

"There is a great and exciting movement in the world of science to look at the possibility of creation with a scientist's eye. Our schools need to be progressive enough to show that to the students. We need to embrace this dispute and admit there is no theory that's been proven to be correct. We need to teach the students to use their own minds to judge what's reasonable. That's what education is in its best form. That's the higher standard we need to strive for.

"Now, there's a lot more I could say, but I've been asked to be brief. I just hope you'll keep in mind what I've said. I wasn't running roughshod over the curriculum content. I was respectful of the theory presented in the text, and I only offered an alternative." Turning back to the head table, he concluded, "I stand with a very good record of complying with the authority of the school board. I'm asking them to stand behind me now."

Once he had taken his seat again, the microphone was opened to anyone in the audience to make comments. Here, the orderliness began to break down.

"I just want to say that I don't personally have anything against Mr. Shepherd or what he said in class. It's just that if we allow him to teach whatever he wants to the kids, then we've got to do the same for every other nut who comes along. There are enough weird notions coming home with my children from school. I don't think it's wise to open up another can of worms. And, well, that's all I've got to say."

"He didn't do anything wrong, as I see it," one of the fathers was explaining.

"He was preaching! That's not okay with me," a woman called from the back of the room.

"Please, please." Henley was tapping his gavel on the table. "We need to do this in an orderly fashion. Kindly respect everyone else in the room by speaking in turn. You'll all get a chance."

"If you're going to force us to take all mention of God out of our schools," the father continued, now turning back toward the woman who had spoken up, "you're going to have to rewrite the Declaration of Independence, our Constitution, and pretty much every other major document prior to the last couple of decades."

"Then let's do it. We don't need religious crutches anymore."

Before Henley had had a chance to object, the father was responding. "Religion isn't a crutch. It makes up the very timbers that our country was built upon. Is that what you want to throw away?"

Again Henley tapped the gavel. "Thank you, Mr. Leeson. Next."

"I'll tell you what he's doing. He's protecting our right to freedom of religion. That's what he's doing. He's standing up for his constitutional rights. You can't throw him out of our school for talking about his religion. It's out-and-out unconstitutional."

"He shouldn't even be teaching. He's telling the kids some kind of fable about the world being made by some unseen god, and we're sitting around asking each other if we should let him teach the same stuff again. What in the world is he doing in the classroom at all? That's what I want to know."

Jon's heart sank as he listened and watched. The communication gap in the room was widening, the issue becoming less defined with every word.

Two hours later it was over. Jon tossed the car keys onto the kitchen counter and slumped onto the couch. He had lost. He had expected that. So why was it that he felt emotionally beaten by the experience? As a tenured employee, the school board couldn't officially release Jon from his employment until they had proven his wrongdoing in a court of law. Of course, he could resign, and, though he would likely never teach again, at least he could move forward with his life. Or he could dive into the court case and hope to come out intact. As much as he had prepared for this moment, the decision would not be an easy one.

# Thirteen

*Monday, May 10*

Ever since her fight with Neal, Esther had backed away from almost all issues in editorial meetings. It wasn't that she was giving in to his implied threat—either that Watt was coming close to the end of his patience with her or that Neal would withdraw his hand of protection from her. It was simply that she hadn't yet been able to reason out her best course of action. It seemed wise to let things cool down for a while, and the reporter instinct she had nurtured in the past few years told her to stay close enough to the source of her troubles to gather more information before deciding how to react. She had no idea what Watt might owe Neal. It seemed most obvious that Neal had been the one to help him obtain his position at this station.

It had been a huge relief for Esther that Watt had decided against sending her to the Shepherd hearing. He had intended to have her there—had even made plans so that she'd be available—but, in a stroke of luck that Esther was sure could only have been heaven sent, there had been "more important dogs to chase"—as Watt had been so eloquent in pointing out. But the story could not be avoided any longer. She had kept up with it as it had unraveled, had even tracked down the additional information that she felt would be pertinent, but, at the same time, she had been grateful not to have been asked for her updates thus far.

"Okay, that schoolteacher's going to court. It was announced over the weekend. He kept us in suspense for more than three weeks. Don't tell me he hasn't got a strategy to groom this news story for all it's worth." Watt was openly watching for Esther's reaction. "So, Branson, what have you got for us to air?"

Esther forced a smile and plunged in. "There's no indication that he's hired legal counsel yet, though he's sure to do so before long. Several local churches have taken up his case and are coming out strongly in support of him. Apparently there's also a Christian research center in Colorado backing him—providing financial support, though I'm not certain of how much."

"Okay." Watt seemed ready to tackle the story now. Esther studied his face as he spoke. "Get that organization on the phone and get some answers from them. What do we need? Let's see. We need to know who they are, what they do, why they're interested in him, how they found out about him, and who's footing the bills for his legal fees. Anything else?"

"Are you looking for a phone interview or footage?" Esther ventured.

"Both," came Watt's response, "though the footage can come from our network affiliate station in the area."

"I can help." Steve had seemed interested in this story from the start.

"No . . ." Watt allowed a pregnant pause. "This story stays with Esther."

Silence fell around her. Even the shuffling papers were still.

"All right," she answered evenly. "I'll do it."

Immediately after the meeting, Esther set out. If this was to be a test of her skills as an unbiased reporter, then she was ready. Watt would get his story, as well as any interesting tidbits she could dig up along the way. Neal may have put her in front of the camera, but she was determined to keep herself there.

Slowly, Esther pieced together information about the research center. She spoke with several researchers and also with secretaries at a couple of the sponsoring organizations. Everything she found impressed her. The people she spoke with were very willing to give her the information she was seeking, and more besides.

The most profitable conversation was with a Dr. Lloyd Finley. Esther learned that he had been Jon Shepherd's contact at the center, and she obtained details about a tour he had been given earlier that spring. She was surprised to hear that Mr. Shepherd had not been associated with Dr. Finley prior to that time.

Without much difficulty, Esther gathered answers to each of Watt's questions. Once again, by the time she received her copy of the evening script, it was obvious the piece had been shortened. However, she glanced through the edits made to her work and found with relief that it had not been rewritten to be slanted. Of course, Esther knew how carefully she had worked to keep it unbiased. She had even been afraid it would become too bland to be aired, but apparently Watt had decided to simply shorten it.

With a sigh of relief, Esther headed down to the makeup chair she knew was waiting. *Perhaps the storm at work has passed.*

❧ ❧ ❧ ❧

"There were four more messages today, Jon. Are you ever going to let one of those television stations interview you?"

Jon shrugged. "Why?"

"People are going to think you're scared . . . or that you have something to hide."

"I don't think it'll do any good. And isn't there some kind of biblical principle against that? Something about the wise man not stepping into traps that are set for him. Or not throwing pearls to pigs?"

Caleb wasn't buying his defense. "You're just chicken."

"Okay, then *you* go."

"I get your point." But Caleb was laughing at him just the same.

"I wish they'd just quit calling. I can't even watch the news without seeing 'my story' discussed by people who didn't care who I was last week. And you know what?" Jon turned to face Caleb. "This morning I went into a grocery store, and this lady kept looking at me. Every time I turned down another aisle, there she was. She even got in line behind me, like she was checking out my groceries, seeing what I was buying. Can you believe that?"

"That's the high price you pay for being famous."

"Infamous is more what I'm feeling." Then Jon's voice lowered. "They're calling the youth center now, too. Somebody got the number and they're calling continually. June's ready to stop answering the phone."

"Maybe you should talk to somebody, Jon. Maybe if you give them what they want they'll leave you alone."

"I'll think about it. But, man, I *really* hate the idea."

❧ ❧ ❧ ❧

The following morning, just as Esther had rinsed her empty juice glass and set it in the kitchen sink, the telephone rang. To her delight, it was her grandfather.

"Oh, it's so good to hear your voice. How are you, Granddad?"

"I'm fine, child—and yourself? How is work going?"

"It's good. I've settled back in. And it's going well."

"Fine. Fine." He cleared his throat as if feeling awkward. "Now, Esther, I'd like to ask you about our discussion. I have wanted to call each day since you left, but I felt it was better to give you some time without a nosy grandfather pushing in."

"You're not nosy at all. And I feel wonderful! It's like I'm a different person," Esther gushed to him.

"I'm so pleased for you."

"I've been reading my Bible every day. And I've been learning so much. All those stories I thought I understood had meanings I never even guessed at." It was so good to have someone she could talk to, openly and without restraint, about her budding faith. She hadn't realized how badly she had been craving that Christian contact.

"That's good. It's so important to give yourself ways to grow and learn. Have you also been attending church somewhere?"

This answer came more slowly. "I've tried. But the nearest church is very different from the one back home. I feel so awkward. I just don't fit in."

"Don't the people there make you feel welcome, dear?"

Esther thought about all the warm smiles she had received. "They do—at least, they try. It's me, I guess. I really wanted to find the kind of church I grew up in. That's silly, I suppose. I just wish I could fly home every Sunday."

"Esther"—his rebuke was patient and kind—"you're not a little girl anymore. You live in Atlanta and you need to find church friends there. I can't tell you how important it is for someone in your position—someone who has recently been saved—to go to church. Not because it will make you 'holy' to do so, but because you need to be together with other believers. You need to learn from them and be accountable to them. It's not intended to be just a new circle of friends. It will help to keep your convictions strong. Satan would like to trip you up now. And if you are alone, it will be very easy for him to do so. Don't leave yourself unguarded."

Esther had listened with rapt attention. It had never occurred to her that she *needed* to be with other Christians. "I'll go, Granddad. I promise, I'll go."

"Good. Good. I know you will. Now let's move on to more pleasant conversation. How is Neal? I suppose you had a chance to tell him, too."

Esther's joy that Granddad had called was wearing thin. This would be a very difficult topic to discuss. "He wasn't exactly elated. He doesn't understand what all the fuss is about, and he always thought my morals were a little too rigid, anyway." Esther cringed. That was more than she had wanted to admit to Granddad. Silence followed.

"What has he said to you about it?" He quickly followed with, "If you don't want to talk with me about this, Esther, I understand."

"It's okay." She was beginning to realize that he was the only person in her life she could trust for advice. As difficult as this was to discuss, she knew she had better do her best to be honest. "Uh, he's basically not very happy with me right now. But that's not because of my decision. He's concerned that I'm causing trouble at work. That I'm trying to be the station's 'conscience.' It's really hard for me to find the right balance. I'm afraid I'm really struggling with that. It's no wonder Neal is having a hard time understanding."

"Hmm." Granddad was offering her no encouragement to feel sympathy for Neal.

"We haven't even spoken for a while. He came over to the house, but we had a big fight and he left."

Granddad was reading between the lines. "This house. Do you live there together?"

"No," Esther was quick to assure him. "No. The house was a gift from Neal, and we *will* live here together after we're married. But he doesn't stay here now. That was our agreement. I was very specific about that."

Granddad seemed to be fumbling for a comment that wouldn't dig him deeper into her private life. "A gift of a house. That's a big gift. What's it like?"

"Oh, it's wonderful. It's in a great subdivision with plenty of trees and lots that are—well, pretty big. And the house is great. It's brick, with vaulted ceilings and huge rooms. With just myself kicking around in it, it seems way oversized, but once we're married and settled, I'm sure it will be just right."

"That sounds lovely. I wish I could see it. Perhaps you can send me a picture."

"I'll do better than that." Esther had been struck with an incredible idea. "I'll fly you out here. You can stay for a visit—as long as you like. There's plenty of room. You said you loved traveling to the South in your younger days. The weather's perfect right now, and I have mornings off so we could go places for fun or just sit and talk. Please come, Granddad. It would be so good to have you here."

"I don't think so. I don't take well to flying. I really should stay put."

"Then you could take the bus—or the train. You said you used to love to ride the train. I'm sure we could find you a way to get here. Please come."

He was weakening. Esther could hear it in his thoughtful silence.

"You wouldn't have to stay long. But, then again, you could stay for a couple weeks and really get the feel of Georgia." She was winning. She knew she was.

It wasn't long before he allowed himself to be persuaded to visit. Esther grabbed her calendar from its place on the shelf above the telephone and a pencil from the holder beside it. "When would this work for you? I can be ready for you anytime."

He paused thoughtfully. "I would need to be back before too long."

In no time, the plans were set and Esther was saying good-bye, full of excitement about seeing him so soon. He had agreed to take the bus, saying that the new trains went too fast for him to enjoy them, and Esther placed a call immediately to obtain his ticket. It had never before occurred to Esther to invite him. Now that the idea had surfaced, she was thrilled. It seemed that Monday's arrival would never come.

❧ ❧ ❧ ❧

"Mr. Shepherd, I'm glad to finally meet you. Please, have a seat. Dr. Finley has told me many of the details of your case already, but I'm glad to get a chance to speak with you personally."

Jon looked across the oversized desk at the attorney. This was an opportunity he had not expected—had not requested. The research center had been willing to share a large portion of the legal expenses for his trial. They had found this lawyer and had made the appointment for Jon to meet with him. Such generosity always seemed to raise suspicion in Jon. Had he not already visited the association and met many of its members, he would never have considered the offer. As it stood, Jon sized up the man warily, hoping this lawyer who was to represent him would prove to be a man he could trust.

"May I begin by introducing myself, and answering the obvious question about why I'd like to represent you in this case?"

"Of course." Jon was glad the other man was willing to be direct.

"First of all, I *am* a believer. I make no secret of that in any case I represent. Now, not every lawyer in my company shares this belief, but they are comfortable with it anyway. So it's fairly typical for me to receive cases having to do with Christian issues. There aren't that many, really, but those that arrive in our office are usually delegated to me. And I'm very satisfied with that arrangement.

"For you, this means that I am well acquainted with the legal issues of trials based upon religious freedoms. I have a very good record, and I am pleased with the way my company has stood behind each of my cases."

Jon was still watching him intently.

"I've watched your case closely, Mr. Shepherd, because of the legal issues involved. But also for one other very important reason." He paused. "It just so happens that I have a daughter who attends second grade in the same county in which you were teaching. I have a personal interest in your case, so to speak. I'm sure I don't need to tell you how important she is to me. And how determined I am that she have a proper education. I believe we can win this case."

Jon was convinced now and ready to get to work. "I've made a list of my questions, Mr. Vollman. Can we discuss them now, or is it too early?"

With a smile, the attorney drew a pencil from the holder on his desk and opened a leather notebook laid out in front of him. "There's no reason we can't begin now."

❧ ❧ ❧ ❧

Esther waited inside the bus station, searching for signs that the bus would be on time. It was due in three minutes—she had already been waiting for half an hour, pacing to the windows and back to the seating again while trying not to appear distraught. She was now a little worried that she had encouraged Granddad to travel so far alone.

Suddenly, the rumble of an approaching bus stirred her. It was here. She hustled to the door and out onto the narrow sidewalk. With a lurch and a hiss, the bus pulled up to its yellow line and stopped. Searching each passenger as they disembarked, it was some time before Esther was able to discern Granddad's smiling face from among them. At last he descended, carefully taking each of the oversized steps one at a time. He looked so much older here—and oddly out of place. Esther wished she hadn't been so adamant that he come. Perhaps she had been selfish to ask.

"Esther!" He was calling to her above the drone of the bus engine.

She answered with a smile and an anxious wave.

There followed the hugs of greeting and then the gathering of luggage, all done with the overwhelming noise and fumes of the bus. Esther was so grateful when they were finally walking away from the confusion, carrying his suitcases, arm in his arm. Finally, they could converse.

"How was the trip?"

"Fine. Fine. I met a couple of nice young ladies. They were traveling together on their way to Florida for vacation. Very friendly. Very polite. They taught me a new card game, and I showed them that old trick I used to do for you."

Esther placed the suitcases into her trunk and slammed down the lid. Granddad waited while she scrambled to unlock his door. "It's so warm here for May. I'd forgotten."

"Did you travel here often when you were working for the paper?"

"Oh, here—and everywhere. I traveled so much I lost track of where I've been and when."

"Do you miss it?"

"Oh, that's hard to say. I miss the people—but not the travel, I guess. In fact, I have some old cronies in this area that I plan to call while I'm here. It will be good to see them again, if we can manage it."

"I'm happy you'll get the chance." Esther had always enjoyed hearing Granddad talk about his days as a reporter. In her mind, she could see him so clearly as a young news hound. All the family photo albums boasted of his looks and charm. Esther was so proud of this image of Granddad.

By the time they pulled off the highway, Esther had coaxed Granddad into repeating some of her favorite stories—about interviewing famous people and witnessing major events. She had even had a chance to fill him in on what was transpiring in her relationship with Watt Shreve. He knew the type, he had said. In fact, it was funny—even the name had sounded familiar to him.

"The best thing to do, dear, is keep out from under. Don't go looking for trouble where there's none already. If he's like the rest of those stuffed shirts, he'll be mostly hot air. I wouldn't be worried about him if I were you."

Granddad was so easy to talk to—so calm and consoling—yet Esther was certain he would not restrain himself if he felt he had advice she needed to hear. She had learned that from their last conversation. It made her even more grateful that he was willing to listen. She hoped she would be wise enough to be open with him if further need arose.

As Esther approached her driveway and pushed the button on the garage door opener, she sent a smile in his direction. It was going to be a pleasure to share this visit with him.

"Okay, this is it."

They entered the house together, Esther carrying the heavier suitcase and letting herself ramble about ideas and plans they had for each room as she toured him through her home, finally showing him the room in which he would be sleeping.

"This looks like I've taken your bedroom, child. No, you need to sleep in your own room."

"Oh, it's fine. Really. I'll take the guest room down the hall where my desk is." Esther felt she should explain further. "I just don't have much furniture yet, so I borrowed a cot from Annie and I'm already settled there. I really want you to take the good mattress. That's already decided. I'll have to bother you from time to time to get clothes out of my closet, but other than that I already set everything up."

He patted her cheek and stepped farther into the room.

"I'll have lunch ready for us in just a few minutes," Esther went on. "Would you like to wash up while you're waiting? Or change clothes? I can bring you whatever you need." Esther wanted so much for him to feel at home.

"I believe I *will* change clothes." Then, chuckling softly, he added, "I need to get the trail dust off, but I'll be down shortly for lunch. Thank you."

Esther pulled the door closed behind her with a last smile in his direction.

❧ ❧ ❧ ❧

Esther was grateful that Watt had eased up on her at work. He seemed to be satisfied that she was back under control. That was a relief and made it easier for her to let down the defenses that she had been growing used to needing so that she could relax and enjoy her visit with Granddad. Neal had still not called, though. It had been over a month since their fight, and as angry as Esther still was at him, she expected to be able to patch things up between them.

The most difficult thing about Granddad's visit was the fact that Esther needed to leave him to head for work in the afternoon and she knew she wouldn't be home until after midnight. He assured her over and over that he preferred to spend mornings with her rather than evenings, anyway. He was used to going to bed early. And, besides, he confided that he was looking forward to watching her on the television every night at six. It was the next best thing to having her with him.

By Saturday, they had grown accustomed to having each other around and were able to be relaxed and informal. They decided to spend the day together, driving to see all of the important historical sites in and around Atlanta. Esther normally tried to keep to familiar roads and highways, but together they ventured around the city, exclaiming over what they were seeing and chatting amiably. Granddad was fearless in trying uncharted roads, and he kept coaxing her to take "the scenic route." Esther could only imagine what he had been brave enough to do when he was in the prime of his life. It had been a wonderful day.

"How about another pancake, Granddad?" Sunday had dawned warm and hazy.

"No, dear. No. I've already eaten more this morning than I do all day when I'm at home. You're going to send me back fat and lazy."

"You? Never."

"Let me at least clear the table for you, Esther. I know you still need to shower and dress. Cleaning up is the least I can do after such a good breakfast."

"Well, if you want to. But don't fuss over the kitchen, Granddad. We can always do that when we get back from church." Inwardly, Esther was still not looking forward to revisiting the nearby church. Her only hope was that having him with her would make her feel more comfortable there.

❧ ❧ ❧ ❧

"Tonight will be a special service," the young pastor was announcing. "We are going to be bringing in a schoolteacher, named Jon Shepherd, who will soon be going to court over a discussion he led during a junior high science class. I'm sure many of you have been following this story in the news, and I hope you will be able to attend. I'm told he's very well informed about the issue and that the evening is sure to make us all more aware of our civic rights and responsibilities."

Esther frowned. Had Watt been right in judging this teacher as self-promoting?

Leaning closer, Granddad whispered, "Do you want to go?"

"Home? Now?"

"No. Tonight. To hear that young man speak. I think I'd like to come."

"Yes, I'd like to," she whispered back. Here was a good opportunity for her to gather more information about the teacher. She had to admit that by now she was very interested in seeing this Jon Shepherd and hearing what he had to say for himself. It should be a very enlightening evening.

However, during the afternoon Neal finally called. They had not spoken for so long that Esther found it awkward to do so now. In his most charming manner, Neal invited her to dinner so they could try to make amends. She wasn't sure how to respond. With firm words, Granddad reassured her that he was not disappointed they wouldn't go to the evening service together and encouraged her to meet with Neal—he had no doubt it would be better for them to talk. Esther gave in, despite her misgivings.

❧ ❧ ❧ ❧

"Could you use an arm, sir?" Jon approached the gentleman from below him on the stairs to the church foyer and was already reaching to place a hand under the shaky arm.

"Oh, thank you. Thank you. I was beginning to feel like I was climbing Everest."

"Are you going into the service now?"

"Yes, I'm a little early, I know. But I guess I'll use the extra time to recover from my walk."

"Your walk?" They had reached the top and were moving toward the sanctuary. Jon noted it was easier for the gentleman now that the stairs were behind them.

"Oh, my granddaughter lives nearby and I thought I would have no trouble walking the short distance. It's amazing how much older this body is than it feels when I'm rested and looking for something to do."

"Did she come with you—your granddaughter, that is? I take it you live with her."

The lanky gray-haired man lowered himself onto a padded pew. "No, I'm visiting from Nebraska. Just here for a couple of weeks or so. We were in church this morning together, but Esther had somewhere to be tonight. I didn't tell her I was planning to come without her. She may have canceled her plans and that would have been a shame." Having settled himself comfortably on the seat, he added warmly, "Thank you again, son. I appreciate your concern. And I guess I should introduce myself." He lifted a hand toward Jon. "I'm Morris Branson."

"It's good to meet you, Mr. Branson. I'm Jon Shepherd." He shook the offered hand.

"Well, then. You must be the young man I've come to hear speak. Is that so?"

"I guess it is. I hope it'll be worth your trouble." Looking up, Jon spied Caleb sitting in a nearby pew alone. "Mr. Branson, there's someone I'd like to introduce you to. Caleb, can you come over here?"

Caleb rose and moved toward them cordially. "Mr. Branson, this is my brother Caleb. He's come along with me tonight for moral support. I'm afraid I'm not much of a speaker, so I have to plant him in the audience to have somebody who'll laugh at the right times. I was hoping I could introduce the two of you so you could each have someone to sit with."

"It's nice to meet you, Caleb. I'd appreciate the company."

"Mr. Branson is from Nebraska. He's visiting his daughter—no, I believe you said your granddaughter."

"Yes. She lives nearby."

Caleb nodded at Jon, who turned and hustled back to where he had been setting up a slide presentation, leaving the two of them to chat together.

Slowly, people began to filter into the church. Then rows began to fill. Soon there were no empty spaces in the vast room and it was time for Jon to be introduced. A hush fell over the sanctuary.

Jon began by explaining the nature and progress of his case. Then, apologizing for the fact that he was a novice in the scientific realm, he explained that his reason for being with them tonight was to share what he had recently discovered for himself. He began a systematic look at what he believed were the fallacies of evolution and the origin of the world theories that most schools espoused.

Flashing across the bright screen, Jon showed slide after slide from various science textbooks available and in circulation. Over and over again, it was the same thing. First, there would be a page explaining that in 1688 Francesco Redi, an Italian physician, had experimented with maggots on meat to show that no maggots formed where flies had not been allowed to reach the rotting tissues. Redi had declared that the people of his day had been wrong in assuming the maggots grew spontaneously out of the meat—"abiogenesis," or life emerging from something that was not alive itself. He proposed from his experiments that living organisms are only produced by other living organisms—"the principle of biogenesis." This principle was usually highlighted in bold letters, sometimes with the text showing condescension to the misinformed people of the day who had believed that the maggots were produced by the rotting meat itself.

Then Jon showed the pages from each textbook that followed closely on the heels of the introduction to Redi's work. Time and again, each book abandoned Redi's findings and declared that life on earth had originated from a primordial soup, which had contained the necessary chemical composition to generate life. Jon paused. "Here are two contradicting statements from the same *chapter* in most textbooks. One says that life never arises from nonliving material, and the next that life evolved from a chemical soup with a little electricity thrown in. Is this the science that we are being asked to embrace and to repeat to students without question? Is this what educated people of the twentieth century—or very soon the twenty-first century—are expected to accept as fact?"

From there, Jon surveyed each of the issues he felt were stumbling blocks as quickly as he could explain them. From the lack of links along the proposed evolutionary ladder to the difficulties with various forms of dating prehistoric artifacts and fossils; from the failure of thousands of scientists to ever produce a genetic mutation of a fruit fly that was a different species than its parents, though this had been attempted for decades the world over, to the mathematical impossibility that even the human eye could have been developed by chance. Here Jon stopped to read a quotation from Charles Darwin himself, taken directly from his famous work, *The Origin of Species.*

" 'To suppose that the eye with all its inimitable contrivances for adjusting the focus to different distances, for admitting different amounts of light, and for the correction of spherical and chromatic aberration, could have been formed by natural selection, seems, I freely confess, absurd in the highest degree.' " Jon set his notes down on the podium.

"Ladies and gentlemen, we often spend a great deal of time and effort trying to justify or disprove what common sense tells us plainly. Even Darwin knew that his theory had points at which it stumbled miserably. Now let me read what the Bible says.

"Romans 1:20. 'For since the creation of the world God's invisible qualities—his eternal power and divine nature—

have been clearly seen, being understood from what has been made, so that men are without excuse.'

"Not everyone *will* see. For whatever reason, we can choose to be blind. But the evidence is there—whether you're looking through a microscope in a laboratory or at the grandeur of the Rocky Mountains. God can be seen clearly if we are willing to look.

"Now, I'm sure that to many of you these failures in the theory of evolution are not new information. For that, I apologize. It's likely you've heard all of this before from someone far more proficient in telling it than I am. But let me go a step further tonight.

"Let me introduce you to some of the work of men and women around the world who are looking at the theory of creation with a scientist's eye. There are many of us who are not aware of current studies and writings; certainly, I wasn't until recently."

Jon could feel his pulse quicken now. This was what he had wanted for so long—this chance to share what he had been discovering. With colorful slide pictures and charts, Jon took his audience through the latest theories of creation scientists. Interweaving Bible passages, historical accounts from all around the globe, and modern research projects, he watched as faces around him were drawn into expressions of awe at what he was showing them.

Here, for their own examination, was a picture of a fossilized tree trunk, stretching through several layers of strata. "This shouldn't be," Jon gushed. "If each of these layers was formed independently, a trunk like this could never exist. If it were deposited with the first layer, all of the wood that was above that ground would have rotted away long before other layers would have formed around it—that is, if it took thousands of years to make the layers. The only explanation for this tree is that all of these layers formed at once.

"Now let's look at animal fossils." Here Jon displayed evidence that had been unearthed showing woolly mammoths in Arctic areas and drew their attention to the implications. It was a heady feeling for Jon. His audience was clearly moved. People were listening to what he had to say as idea after idea was laid out in his presentation. Checking his watch, he knew he would soon need to close. He switched off the light on the overhead projector with disappointment that he had not gotten through all that he had hoped to present.

"Let me try to explain, in closing, what I wanted to accomplish by coming here tonight and what I have discovered from my years spent teaching. There are many truly devoted Christians in our schools today who have been convicted to action over the lack of morals our society has encouraged our children to embrace and the resulting difficulties they endure because of it. From crisis pregnancies to illicit drug use and violence, our schools are a breeding ground for moral atrocities. And make no mistake—it *is* the youth of America who are bearing the pain of the wounds that we as adults have allowed to fester. I applaud these courageous people—the ones hard at work with our young people. They are a lifeline to so many children who need them.

"But I have chosen—or perhaps been given—a different fight right now. I have chosen to stand against the lie that we are products of chance, and the loss of hope that belief brings. You see, many of the problems in our schools grow from the inability to admit that there is such a thing as sin—as behavior that always produces undesirable consequences. We can never forget that the whole reason God says 'Thou shalt not . . .' is to prevent us from hurting ourselves and those around us. God's law is never arbitrary. It is never a random denial of wholesome activities.

"But evolution, and its accompanying scientific ideas, goes a step further, beyond denial of sin. It denies God himself. Stop for a minute and let that sink in. Your children, our next generation, are being told day after day in almost every classroom across America that there is no God! Do we understand the significance of that to our society? Can we imagine all the implications? I don't think we really do, but I know we've been living with them for almost a century. We have suffered through the degradation of life itself, the devaluation of the home and family, the denial that there is any type of higher law or duty—all, at least partly, because we have allowed God to be discarded. If there is no God, there is no reason for my existence—I am a product of chance. If there is no God, I am answerable to no higher authority—I am my own authority, choosing actions which are in my own best interests as I see them. To me, this is the most grievous kind of miseducation going on in our schools."

Jon paused and surveyed his audience. "I'm here because this is my battle now. I took up this fight when I refused to buckle to the idea that beliefs that oppose evolution have no place in a schoolroom. And, God helping me, I will not give in until I have done everything in my power to be heard.

"Now I'm asking for your help. I'm aware that you feel like you're being pressed in on all sides to get involved with one issue or another. And I've learned from experience that we're each chosen to accomplish different purposes. But if you are listening and you feel like this might be an area where God wants you to join the battle, I want to help you know where to start.

"One of the best things you can do is to know your own school system, meet with your principal, and attend school board meetings. Be a homeroom helper or a library assistant. Find out when textbooks and curricula are approved and get onto the committee to review them—that's vital. I know we're all busy. The last thing we want is more on our schedules. But don't allow yourself to fall into the habit of choosing the everyday over the eternal. If God is calling you to stand in the gap, be faithful. We need moms and dads, aunts and uncles, and grandparents who are willing to be watch-dogs for our kids.

"We also need people who will go a step farther." Again Jon paused and searched the eyes of those looking up at him.

"I'm learning a lot during this period of suspension. I'm learning that there are some very conflicting ideas about how to interpret Genesis. I was raised on this story. I thought it was pretty straightforward—I had no idea how many questions and implications it raises.

"But I spoke with a German scientist, an older man who had seen a lot of theories come and go in his day. He brought it all into focus for me. You see, it's tempting to look at the different theories of creation science and argue those. That's what I started out looking for. I read all the books, ready to choose which one I'd be willing to embrace. Are we on an old planet or a young one? How old are the stars? When were the ice ages?

"But we can't—for the sake of our children we *must not* allow such questions to divide us or deter us from the real fight. We're not against one another. We're against the ones who say there is no God—there is no place for a Higher Power in an educated world. We're against their stranglehold on education that allows them to teach this to our kids.

"In the book of John, Jesus prays in a radical way. Let me read it for you. 'My prayer is not for them alone. I pray also for those who will believe in me through their message, that all of them may be one, Father, just as you are in me and I am in you. May they also be in us so that the world may believe that you have sent me. I have given them the glory that you gave me, that they may be one as we are one: I in them and you in me. May they be brought to complete unity to let the world know that you sent me and have loved them even as you have loved me. Father, I want those you have given me to be with me where I am, and to see my glory, the glory you have given me because you loved me before the creation of the world.'

"Are we living examples of this prayer? Do we come together as believers in unity, strength, and glory because of His power and His ultimate message of hope? That is God's clear intention for us. We need to pray Christ's prayer on our own behalf. Please join me in praying for that as we close."

Granddad had listened carefully to all that Jon had said. Most of it had been new ideas for him. In the quietness of his heart he considered the words. He thought about the children. He thought about their homes. He thought about the difficult world that they had been given to grow up in. Tears gathered in his eyes as he rubbed his softening hands against one another, wondering what work they would still be able to accomplish before he passed on—what role he could take.

When Jon had descended from the platform and managed to weave through the sanctuary after pausing to speak with each person who introduced themselves, he was disappointed to find that Morris Branson was already gone.

"I didn't even see him leave," Caleb answered his unspoken question. "I got talking and just didn't see him leave."

Jon peered out toward the door, hoping to catch a glimpse of him. "I had hoped to drive him home. I should have offered before the meeting even started. . . ." Feeling a pat on his shoulder, he was drawn into another conversation.

# Fourteen

*Sunday, May 23*

Esther and Neal had found a feeble peace, though there were many questions she couldn't form aloud. The old Neal was back, though. He had smiled and even laughed, but Esther felt a nagging twinge of fear as she said good-night. She locked the door behind her and could tell that Granddad had gone to bed. Tiptoeing past his door and into the spare room, she flopped down on Annie's cot. It was a relief to see that her guest had been fine while she was gone.

On Monday morning, Esther rose as usual and began cooking breakfast for the two of them. Granddad had already taken his favorite seat on the porch, his Bible lying open on his lap, his eyes closed in prayer.

"Esther, may I speak with you?"

She set the bubbling oatmeal on the back of the stove and walked out to where he was seated. "Of course, Granddad. You know you can."

"First of all, I have a little confession to make. I hope you won't be upset."

Esther smiled. What could he possibly do to upset her?

"I walked to the meeting last night."

She frowned. "The one at the church?"

"I walked over to hear what the schoolteacher had to say."

"You *walked*? It's too far. I would have taken you. If you wanted to go, why didn't you ask? Granddad, I would have taken you."

"I was fine. It isn't far. And that's not even why I'm starting this conversation. I want to talk with you about what was said."

Esther was clothed in guilt that she had abandoned him. She wasn't ready to move on in their discussion yet. "I'm so sorry. I didn't know how badly you wanted to go."

"Please, dear. Please. Listen to what I'm saying. I want to talk about the meeting." As quickly as possible, he gave a summary of the presentation. Gradually, she began to leave behind her shock that he had gone without her and was drawn into what he was saying.

"I believe in Jon Shepherd's fight. I believe he is a good man—a man of God who has been called for this purpose. He spoke with honesty and intensity and . . . well, with fire. And yet, he portrayed genuine love for the children. He does love the children, Esther. That was so very apparent."

He concluded with even more surprising news. "I have prayed and prayed since last night. And I keep coming back to the idea that I have some role to serve in all of this—though I don't know what that might be."

Esther studied his face. He was very serious. She had not seen him as resolute as he was now.

"I want to ask if I could stay a little longer with you." His eyes rose to meet hers.

Esther broke into a wide smile. "Oh, yes! Oh, Granddad, I want you to stay for as long as you can. I feel badly because I don't think I'm taking care of you the way I should be, heading out the door to go to work all the time, but I definitely want you to stay as long as you can. I love having you here. I love getting to know you better and sharing this big empty house with you. It's been more wonderful having you here than I can even say.

"And as far as Jon Shepherd goes, I'll help you in any way I can. I've been covering the story at the station, and I'd be happy to pass along what information I glean."

It was settled, then. Granddad would stay.

❧ ❧ ❧ ❧

Mornings with Granddad and afternoons and evenings at work melted together until another week had passed. They were still enjoying each other, still finding interesting conversations and activities to share, but there was something increasingly strange about Granddad. Esther could tell that his mind was often drifting—seemingly somewhere else. And she noticed that he had started to refer to telephone calls and conversations with old news associates. She wasn't sure whether he was merely renewing old acquaintances or somehow working toward helping Jon Shepherd. It was all Esther could do to keep herself from asking about it, but she decided to wait until Granddad was ready to talk.

Esther spent the last part of Saturday afternoon getting ready for a dinner date with Neal. Though Esther still felt uncomfortable with the role he had played in her promotion, she wasn't able to pinpoint any real wrongdoing and felt hopeful that the whole episode would soon fade from her memory.

Dressed in a pink short-sleeved cotton sweater that had always been Neal's favorite color for her to wear, Esther made her way down the polished staircase. For some reason, she wasn't sure whether she wanted Neal to meet Granddad. As usual, her grandfather seemed to be able to read her thoughts.

"You look very nice, Esther. He's a lucky man. But you've been very fidgety today. Perhaps you feel I won't make a good impression?" There was a twinkle in his eye.

"You? Who could help but love *you*? No. It's just . . . well,

I wish you could have met him a couple months ago, when we were getting along so well. Before all of this mess at the station. He's really a very wonderful man."

He patted her hand and smiled. "I trust your judgment, dear."

Neal arrived at her front door exactly when he had promised. Granddad waited in the kitchen while she went to answer his knock. It seemed so strange for Neal to knock before entering. Esther's hand was as cold as ice as she reached to open the door for him.

"Hi, gorgeous." The first thing Esther saw were the flowers—pink roses—her favorite. Next, her eyes recognized the clean lines of his dark blue double-breasted suit. Esther had always liked this one best, and seeing him standing there tonight in the glow of the porch light, she was certain he had never looked better.

*Okay. Give the guy a fair chance. He's obviously going to great lengths to woo me.* Then Esther met his eyes. He was back. The Neal she had fallen in love with had arrived tonight. His eyes were glowing warmly and his breathtaking smile was almost more than she could bear. While she stood dazed, he stepped inside the room and kissed her gently on the forehead. Time seemed to have stalled, and the only thought in Esther's mind was that he was even wearing her favorite cologne.

"I love you, darlin'," he whispered against her hair.

If it had not been for a sudden clatter from the kitchen, Esther was sure she would have forgotten Granddad entirely.

She pushed herself back from his embrace. "We need to go meet Granddad. I mean, I need to introduce you to him. That is, would you like to meet him?"

"Of course. I want to meet all the important people in your life."

"Granddad, this is Neal." Esther glowed, stumbling for a better way to make the introduction but unable to come up with much. Finally, she managed to add lamely, "And, Neal, this is . . . my granddad."

Neal extended his hand toward the elderly man and Granddad returned the handshake. Esther seemed to be the only one failing to feel composed about their meeting.

"It's nice to meet you, Mr. Branson."

"Morris. Please, call me Morris. It's good to meet you, too. Esther has told me so much about you."

Esther smiled, turning from one to the other.

"I'm glad you've had this chance to visit. You're the first family member to see our new house. I know it means a great deal to Esther to have you here."

"It's a beautiful house. I've been most comfortable. And Esther is a wonderful hostess. I couldn't ask for better care. I just won't know what to do with myself once I'm home again."

"I'm sure that's true. She's a very special person."

Conversation seemed to have ground to a halt. "Well . . ." Neal was ready to move on with his evening plans. "We'd better be going. We have reservations, so we don't want to be late. It was very good to meet you, Morris. I'm sure we'll see each other again soon."

"Yes," Granddad answered. "I'm certain we will."

Taking Esther's arm, Neal walked her into the front hallway and escorted her out the door into the warm evening air.

❧ ❧ ❧ ❧

"Esther, are we doing the Bergman story tonight or was that the one we cut?" Steve Forelli had caught her attention just as she was coming out of makeup.

"No, we cut the other one."

"Okay. By the way . . ." Esther could tell Steve wanted more than an answer about the evening's stories. "I couldn't help but notice a little tension between you and Watt."

"Tension?" Esther wasn't sure if it was wise to admit to any of her co-workers that there were problems.

"Look, I know he can be hard to work with, but you're a really good co-anchor. I enjoy working with you and I don't want to see you miss out on a great opportunity here. Maybe I'm reading in more than what I'm seeing, but for what it's worth, I just wanted to say it's better to let sleeping dogs lie. Guys like Watt are a dime a dozen in this business. He doesn't have much of a future and he knows it. You're something special, though. Don't let him wreck your shot at a good career."

Even though Esther was taken aback by his uncharacteristic comments, she appreciated Steve's candor. It was kind of him to have spoken up.

"I'm sure you're right. I'll do my best."

"Good for you." Steve took a quick look over his shoulder before continuing. "There's one more thing. You should know that you're going to end up covering the Shepherd trial. I'm not sure why Watt's singled you out for that, but it's coming your way just the same."

"Oh, Steve, I really don't want to cover that trial." Esther groaned inwardly at the thought. "I thought I'd done enough with that story now that it's no longer 'human-interest fluff' to Watt."

"I know, but I don't think you're going to get a choice." Steve patted her on the shoulder, then turned back toward the set.

Esther could feel tension rising along the back of her neck. She had fought against a sinking feeling for some time that the trial would end up in her lap just as the hearings had, no matter how much she tried to avoid it. Still, she had no doubt that Steve's instincts were correct.

# Fifteen

*Tuesday, June 8*

The date for Jon Shepherd's trial appeared on the kitchen calendar. Esther gathered the things she would need to make notes of the trial and reached for her car keys and purse, readying herself for a long, tedious day.

"Esther?"

She was sure she knew Granddad's question before he even phrased it.

"I know you will be there on business, but I would really like to go with you to the courthouse today. I don't think this is something I should miss."

Esther knew immediately that it would be useless to argue, just as she knew it was pointless to protest Watt's decision yesterday to make her cover the trial for the station.

She had attended only a few trials while working as a street reporter. Now that she had moved to the anchor desk, she could already tell she had lost a little of her confidence in putting herself into the heart of the action. As she and Granddad walked into the courtroom to watch Jon Shepherd's trial, she felt strangely as though they were sneaking in where they did not belong—as if someone were going to ask her for a hall pass and she'd have none to show. She chose seats far to one side of the courtroom and waited for the proceedings to begin.

Moments before the judge was to arrive, a young man accompanied by two older gentlemen entered from a side door and took their seats at the table assigned to the defense. Esther surveyed them.

"That's Mr. Shepherd," Granddad informed her. Esther's eyes were riveted on Jon. His name had been familiar to her for so long it seemed. What would he be like—this knight for the cause of religious freedom?

He was tall—a little over six feet, she guessed—but also a little stocky, with an undeniably bookish air about him. The blazer and tie that he wore over his blue oxford shirt were outdated and, clearly, uncomfortable for him. Several times while they waited for the judge, Esther noticed him tug nervously at the collar. His dress pants were plain, and on his feet were a pair of well broken-in tennis shoes. Esther wondered why someone hadn't given him a little advice about how to dress for court.

His mannerisms, too, spoke volumes to Esther: the way he slouched slightly in his chair; the way his feet seemed too much in the way no matter where he positioned them under the table; the way he kept his notebook in front of him on the table, seeming to protect it or draw courage from it. Esther wasn't sure which was more true.

But there was also a gentleness to him, and Esther was pleasantly surprised to notice it. The soft waves of hair that tousled around his face, looking just a little unkempt, betrayed a spark of stubbornness in his pensive expression and gentle brown eyes. Perhaps she was projecting some of her own feelings about the case onto the schoolteacher, but Esther felt drawn to him, as if he were someone she would like to know. Immediately, she dismissed these thoughts as having to do with her sympathies about his situation.

But, projections or not, Esther found herself wishing him well as he stood for the entry of the judge and the trial preamble. The proceedings began with the opening remarks of the opposing counsels.

"Mr. Shepherd, who is seated here before you, is a good man." The prosecuting attorney was playing his words skillfully, gesturing toward Jon and turning to the jury with a patronizing air. Esther was certain he would have gone so far as to pat the defendant on the back had he been within easy reach. "He is considered by all around him to be a pillar of the educational profession. We need men like Jonathan Shepherd in our schools today. We need his courage and his ideals. We need his passion for the youth of our city and the concern he feels over their education.

"Ladies and gentlemen of the jury, we have no argument with the character of this man—this fine young schoolteacher. We bear him no malice. In fact, we are remiss that he has lost so much time by being absent from his classroom. So, should the defense attorney attempt to portray the case as being against the shining character of this man, please be forewarned, that is not the issue we are presenting here at all.

"No, the issue is far larger than any one man. The issue is deeply rooted in our country's very constitution and the freedoms it represents. We *have* religious freedom in America. Jon Shepherd is free to choose whatever religious beliefs he feels best suit him. That is his right as an American. For that right, we are all grateful.

"But what about little Susie who sits in Mr. Shepherd's class? Her parents have instructed her at home with one set of religious beliefs. Then Mr. Shepherd clouds those beliefs by projecting upon her his own. Poor little Susie, all she thought she'd be learning in science class was—*science.* Philosophy isn't written into the curriculum. It was never intended to be discussed."

Esther was watching Jon Shepherd carefully. From her seat far to the side, she could see his eyes flash, as if his mind were racing with responses to the prosecutor's remarks. The idea that he might be easy prey—like a deer in the headlights—was leaving her quickly. He had evidently come with every conviction that he could win. His rapt attention to the prosecutor's words was proof.

Esther forced her thoughts back onto what the prosecutor was saying. "We will show Mr. Shepherd to be . . . not of ill intent, but of poor judgment. We will show that his attempts to educate these students to his own religious biases had no place in a classroom supported by public funds—by funds taken from atheists, Baptists, Muslims, Catholics, Jews—all religions together, and none held in esteem or given more authority than any other. Thank you."

Then the defense attorney rose as the legal baton was passed. "Members of the jury, first I would like to thank you for setting aside this time from your busy lives to serve here today. It should prove to be a very interesting trial. We *do* live in a country of freedom, largely because we have each taken part in the responsibility of protecting it. By serving on this jury, you are contributing to the order and justice in our nation. And we appreciate your being here.

"Now then, you've heard the words of Mr. DeFranco. They sounded very good—they seemed to make a great deal of sense—but I want to make you aware of a very important concept in this trial. And that is 'paradigm.' It's a three-dollar word—doesn't come up much in everyday conversation—but it has everything to do with us now. If you'll bear with me, I'll define it as best I can so that there's no confusion as I incorporate it into my remarks.

"Paradigm is how each of us thinks—how each individual interprets the events happening around him every day. Everything that happens—what you see and hear and read—passes through your particular point of view. It's a little like eyeglasses." The attorney held up his own. "If my glasses are tinted, my eyes see the world a little less brightly than what it truly is. If my glasses are a good prescription, I see more clearly and the images are sharper. On the other hand, if my prescription is poor, my view of the world is distorted. Paradigm is my own idea of what the world is like.

"Now let's take that concept and apply it here, to this trial. I'd like you to ask yourself this: Is it the goal of education to present facts, and just the facts, aiming to display no particular paradigm or way of interpreting them? Are we seeking teachers who have an ability to turn off their own way of looking at the world and present lessons devoid of all interpretation? Is that what we want?

"No. No, of course not. No human could do such a thing. Every teacher in whose classroom you have ever seated your child has a particular paradigm. It comes through in the way papers are graded or how test questions are phrased, how lectures are presented, or even which topics are given the most emphasis in the course. There is not one teacher in America today who is able to take his interpretation of the world—his paradigm—and keep it from affecting the way he teaches." He was searching each jury member's face for acknowledgment.

"Jon Shepherd cannot be on trial for what every teacher in America today presents in every lesson that is taught. We cannot attempt to legislate the absence of a person's right to his own point of view from any occupation or situation in the United States." He smiled as he added, "Including jury duty. To do so amounts to legally swinging at shadows; our only choice, then, is to mold our public environments to be accepting of and not offensive to the paradigms represented by our citizens. We will clearly show in our defense how this does not conflict with anything my client said or did in his classroom.

"Now with that foundation firmly in place, I want to quickly summarize the second point we plan to make in this trial—that the theory of evolution is, in fact, a paradigm of its own. It is *not* scientific fact as many school textbooks in the last few decades have touted it to be.

"That there are fossils embedded in rock all around our planet is a fact. That there are exposed layers of earth strata is a fact. That there were once enormous animals we commonly refer to as dinosaurs that lived and died on our earth is also a fact. But the interpretation of these facts to form a theory called 'evolution' is clearly, and without any discrepancy to the well-defined realm of true science, a step beyond fact and into interpretation. The Theory of Evolution by its very definition has not been proven. If it had, it would now be called the Law of Evolution. And all of the remaining questions about its validity would have been answered. Ladies and gentlemen, the Law of Gravity is no longer a theory. The Laws of Physics, as stated by Sir Isaac Newton, are no longer theories. Evolution is still open for dispute, even though scientists all around the globe have scrambled for over a century to prove it and eliminate the remaining questions.

"I ask you, members of the jury, to rise above that part of your own education that probably held out evolution to you as being undisputed fact, and see it now with a scientist's eye. I believe you will see that my client's offering of a scientifically based theory is no different than the offering of the Theory of Evolution in our schools. And that, so long as both theories attempt to sink roots into the facts as we have discovered them so far, each falls into the acceptable content of a science class. Both theories are indeed a step beyond what has been proven and each is an attempt at interpreting the known facts. Each tries to answer one of the biggest questions that we as humans grapple with: How did we come to be? How was everything in our world formed?

"Your answer to these questions may already be established in your own mind. That is not what is on trial. It is the fact that a quality education does not stifle one theory in favor of another *theory*—as long as both fall into the realm of true science. And we will show you, perhaps for the first time in your own experience, how easily and completely the Theory of Creation fits into the established facts drawn from the world around us. Thank you." The defending lawyer took his seat, calm and confident.

Esther drew in a long breath. Well, there it was. The intentions that each lawyer had set out for the trial. There would be no shrinking on either side from the main issue. Creation had been drawn out of the dusty box that had seemingly confined it from the civic eye for so many years. Now it would be marched back and forth across a courtroom. Esther could only hope that the legal system would be open-minded and fair in their treatment of it.

The first task of the trial was to establish exactly what Jon had done on the days when he had taught the science class. Five students were brought forward, each giving a summary of what they believed to have happened. Three could remember Jon explaining the difference between theory and fact clearly—two said they could not. Esther could see Jon squirm in his seat uncomfortably, avoiding eye contact with the students. It seemed to her that the very fact that the teens had been called in at all and asked to testify for or against him was a very difficult facet of the trial for him.

The students were also questioned about how they perceived Jon to have presented the information: Had they felt he was trying to convince them it was correct, or was he simply stating it, as he had claimed? Here, four students testified that he had simply stated the theory and they had not felt he was persuading them to believe it. The fifth student hedged for a moment, and then conceded that she hadn't felt Mr. Shepherd was trying to convince them, either. The prosecutor seemed disappointed but quickly masked his reaction. Esther heard a woman behind her mutter, apparently one of the parents.

Throughout the examination of each student, the defense

attorney seemed to present his side more forcefully that there had been no question as to Jon's motives when he presented the material. Esther was sure the jury had been convinced. That was good. The teacher would, in all likelihood, be able to teach again somewhere—even if he lost his case here.

The questioning of the students, though obviously being done with the greatest of sensitivity, extended on until close to noon. Because of this, when the last youth had stepped down, the judge called a lunch recess until one o'clock.

Esther rose and put her sweater back around her shoulders. She hadn't noticed until now how cool the courtroom was. "I need to make a few phone calls, Granddad. Would you like to come?"

"No, dear. I think I'll stay here. But you go. I'll just sit and ponder what's been said." He smiled up at her.

Esther would only have an hour or two to observe the afternoon's proceedings before she was due back at the news station in order to have time to write up the story. She would be leaving a reporter at the trial to watch for any illuminating statements that might be made after she was gone. It actually might not be worth waiting here until the lunch break was over, but she wasn't sure she could force Granddad to leave before they absolutely had to. She knew he was watching intently.

Following the clusters of people out of the courtroom and into the hallway, Esther pushed past them toward a corridor where she had seen a public telephone. She planned to call her office and listen to her voice-mail messages.

Before she had time to dial, Esther was conscious of another person nearby, apparently waiting to use the telephone. She turned, ready to smile in assurance that she would only be a minute, and stopped short at seeing the defendant himself standing in the corridor.

"H-hello," she stumbled.

"Hi."

"I'll . . . I'll only be a minute."

"That's fine," he assured. "I'm not in a hurry."

Esther smiled weakly and turned to dial the number. Her messages were brief, and hardly more than a hum in her ear now that she realized who was standing behind her. In a moment she placed the receiver back in its cradle, gathered her purse and keys, and turned to go.

"Excuse me," Jon caught her attention. "I couldn't help but notice. You're a news reporter, aren't you? Esther, Esther something . . . is it Brandon?"

"Close." She laughed, surprised that he could be interested in her name at such a stressful time in his life. "It's Branson, Esther Branson. And, yes, I'm a news anchor here in town."

Jon appeared thoughtful for a moment, then asked, "Are you doing a story on the trial?"

Esther immediately realized how her presence must look to him. "Actually, yes. I was assigned to cover your story for our station. But I would have come anyway . . ." Esther wasn't sure how to finish the thought, so she let it hang in the air.

"Just to see what happens?" Jon ended the sentence for her.

"Yes. I guess. Oh, and because my granddad insisted. I think he would have hitchhiked if I hadn't brought him."

"That's it. That's where I've heard the name before. So you must be the granddaughter."

"Excuse me?"

"He was the gentleman who walked over to see me at Palisade Church, right? He came to hear me speak."

"Yes, that's him. That's Granddad. And I'm the horrible granddaughter who took off and didn't even give him a ride over."

Jon laughed. "He didn't say you were horrible."

"He's too forgiving. But he also said some very nice things about you."

"Well, that was generous. I didn't give him a ride, either. I was going to take him home, but he was gone before I was able to ask him."

"He does that." They both laughed and an awkward silence followed. Esther shot a quick glance at her watch and offered, "Well, I'd better get going and let you make your phone call, Mr. Shepherd."

"It was nice meeting you, Miss Branson. And please say hello to your grandfather for me."

"Yes, I'll be sure to do that." Esther stepped past him to allow him to use the phone, then hesitated. Suddenly it became very important to her that she not leave him wondering on which side of the spectator arena she had aligned herself. "Mr. Shepherd, can I say that I, personally, hope you win. You see, I'm a Christian, too." She blushed for a moment and then added, "A fairly new Christian, and I really believe you're doing a good thing by seeing this trial through. It must be an awesome task from where you sit, but I do think . . . that is, I'm convinced God will use it."

Jon had listened carefully as she spoke, smiling in response to her words. "Will you do me a favor?" There was a twinkle in his eye as he asked the question. "Will you be kind to me when you give my story at your station? I need all the friends I can get."

Esther laughed. "Of course I will."

The next session began with little ceremony. With new enthusiasm, Esther studied the cluster of people seated directly behind Jon and concluded that they must be his friends and family. There were other clusters of observers in the room, pockets of people who seemed to belong together. From where she sat, there didn't appear to be many people who had come just for interest's sake. Most seemed to be reporters, parents and students, or school board members and fellow teachers, judging by the things they carried with them and the hushed remarks they made to each other when there was a lull in the proceedings.

"Esther," Granddad whispered hoarsely. "I'd like to stay."

"Okay. We can stay another twenty minutes or so."

"No, dear. I mean, I want to stay even after you have to go to work. I'll take a taxi back if you'll just leave me your house key."

Esther turned to face him. She was about to object, then decided against it. "All right. But will you call me at work as soon as you get back?"

"Of course, child."

The witnesses now were giving testimony about school policy and curriculum evaluations, attempting to define where the current standard lay for what could and could not be presented, and how it had been arrived at. After half an hour of questions, Esther could not postpone her need to leave any longer, so she gestured to Granddad and rose as inconspicuously as possible to head for the parking lot.

In a short time, she found herself back in familiar surroundings. The hush of the courtroom was exchanged for the hustle and high energy of the station, where the afternoon editorial session would soon begin. As she typed up her notes from the afternoon, her mind kept returning to her grandfather sitting at the trial and to Jon Shepherd.

Taking her first opportunity, Esther stopped by to chat with Annie, going over the day's events as she had seen them.

"You met him?" Annie's interest was acute about that point. "What was he like?"

"I don't know. He was nice . . . tall, polite . . . quite private, I think . . . and a bit scruffy."

Annie laughed.

"He did ask me to be kind to him, though," Esther added quickly.

"What?"

"He did! He asked that if I read about him on the news, I would be kind to him."

"And are you thinking that's a little paranoid?"

"Are you kidding? He must have watched his name get smeared in the last couple of months. I'm not surprised he's hoping to find a compassionate soul in the cold world of media." Esther was aware that she was adding a dramatic flare to her answer.

Annie rolled her eyes and turned back toward the tapes she was working over. "What did you tell him?"

"Well, I told him I would."

"What?" Annie was unmoved and blunt. "This guy could be an ax murderer for all you know. I thought you'd seen enough in your time around the news to be a little more guarded about who you believed was a good guy."

Esther frowned. It was true. She had no reason to trust this Jon Shepherd. She had seen some very shady characters turn up behind some very impressive facades, but for some reason she was willing to put her faith in this teacher—at least until someone could prove he had done something wrong. And, too, Granddad had expressed his good feelings about Jon.

"Esther?" Annie's expression showed real concern. "You're not going to do anything stupid, right?"

"Like what?"

"I don't know. Like letting this guy get in the way of your job? You told him you'd be kind to him. What if it turns out he *did* do something wrong and *should* be fired?"

"Then I'll be honest in my story. It doesn't matter what my personal feelings are, Annie. I would be just as honest if he was an ax murderer or a pastor. Right is right. I'm not ever going to hedge on that."

However, the short chat with Annie had cast a shadow over Esther's excitement. As she passed by the closed door of Watt's office, feelings of dread clouded over her once again.

# Sixteen

*Wednesday, June 9*

As morning dawned, Jon rose purposefully—soberly—and began preparing for the trial. He would be taking the witness stand today, perched like a target while all eyes watched to see which lawyer could make the better shots. Of all the instructions he had been given, it bothered him most that he would not be able to take his notes with him. He would be forced to make his rebuttals based only on what he could recall. Moment by moment, through each of the morning activities, Jon sent up short phrases of prayer—for wisdom, courage, and self-control.

As the trial began again, Jon was called forward. The tightness of his chest was almost unbearable, but he rose from his seat and walked toward the bailiff to be sworn in, then stepped up onto the riser and took his seat, looking out over the crowded courtroom, hoping to find a friendly face. Gazing at the sea of faces only made it seem as if the entire world were watching him now.

Mr. Vollman began the questioning. "Mr. Shepherd, please state your full name, occupation, and educational background for the record."

"My name is Jonathan Robert Shepherd. I'm a secondary education teacher with a major in history and a master's degree in education."

"And you work for the public school system of Chattahoochee county. Is that correct?"

"Yes, sir."

"How long have you worked there, Mr. Shepherd?"

"For about four years."

"And when was it that you were suspended from that school system?"

"In February of this year."

Reaching for his notes and walking out in front of the desk, Michael Vollman turned toward the jury. "Can you state for the court the reason for your suspension?"

They had rehearsed Jon's response to this question thoroughly. Trying hard not to sound like he was reciting, Jon answered, "I was suspended for explaining a creation science theory during a class for which I was substitute teaching."

"How many days did you teach that class?"

"Two."

"Did you explain the theory on both days?"

"I only mentioned the theory the first day. I asked if any of the students were aware of it in reference to the material they had been studying. I explained it in detail on the second day."

Jon was already struggling to keep a defensive tone out of his voice and yet remain firm and confident in his answers as he had been instructed. But, in his mind, he wondered how much worse he would be fighting the tension when it was the other attorney asking the questions.

"So the next morning, after researching the topic that night on your own time, what was it that you intended to do with the information?"

"I was going to show the books to Dennis Trent, our principal, and see if he objected to my presenting the material in class."

His lawyer spun back toward Jon quickly. "To present it in class as fact?"

"No, sir. To present it only as a theory."

"Okay. And were you told not to explain the theory?"

"No, sir. Mr. Trent and I weren't able to finish our conversation, so I was told to use my own judgment." Jon's stomach was pinching. He hated feeling as if he were pointing an accusing finger back in Denny's direction. He looked across the rows of onlookers to where he knew Denny was seated, but the man's downcast eyes offered no hint of response.

"Were those his words, Mr. Shepherd? Did he say, 'Use your own judgment'?"

"I don't remember the exact words. But I was told to go ahead with my idea. That Mr. Trent was sure it would be fine."

"And what did you tell the students that day?"

"Well, first I was careful to explain the concept of a scientific theory. That a theory, by definition, has not yet been proven."

"Did you make that statement about the information in the textbook? Did you ever insinuate that it could be wrong?"

Again Jon was careful with his choice of words. "I applied the word 'theory' equally to what was written in the textbook and what I was explaining about the creation science point of view."

Jon could see his lawyer was pleased with the answer.

"And you never made statements that the book was wrong and that, instead, this theory you were introducing was correct?"

In a flash, Jon thought back over all the various ideas he had been exposed to in the last few months. He could feel the emotions surging up inside him. Then he stated, more forcefully than he intended, "I didn't say that then, and I wouldn't say it now. It would have been scientifically unsound to choose *either* theory and try to hold it out as fact.

That was the whole point about spending time first defining with the students what a theory was."

His attorney shot Jon a subtle look that warned, "Back off and calm down."

Jon took a deep breath, determined to control his responses.

Mr. Vollman continued. "So you're saying you did not offer your version of the facts as being correct?"

"No, sir. I did not."

Jon was amazed at how long the questions persisted. They hardly seemed to move forward at all. In no time, a lunch recess was called and Jon retreated from the witness stand, thankful for a reprieve from the stress of testifying.

After the recess, Jon resumed his seat. The courtroom was crowded now, everyone anxious to hear the cross-examination.

"Good afternoon, Mr. Shepherd." Mr. DeFranco approached the witness stand to begin his questioning.

"Good afternoon."

"Let's see. We've established that you are a teacher—and a good one. There's no need to go back over that. We've also established that you were not attempting to convert your students. We've had testimony enough to that fact, as well. But let's chat for a moment about the implications of your words. Do you believe in freedom of religion in the schoolroom?"

"Yes, sir. I do."

"For *all* religions?"

"All religions that are not participating in otherwise illegal activities." Michael had warned Jon about the possibility of having Christianity set up against satanic rituals and occult practices. He had guessed that was where the current questioning was headed.

"Ah, so you're wise enough to rule out those who advocate violence and persecution of other faiths."

Jon wasn't sure what the implications to this question

might be. Certainly, he was aware that Christianity had often fallen into both of those categories in the past. "I don't believe any such practices should be taught in class as honorable or right."

"But you're a history teacher, correct?"

"Yes."

"Then, don't you mention the Crusades, the Spanish Inquisition, or the Jewish conquest of the Promised Land?"

"The study of history is very different from the study of science, Mr. DeFranco. In history, it is appropriate to teach about topics that are considered to be 'failures' or wrong by modern standards. In science, it would be a somewhat meaningless approach to go back over all the inaccuracies of the past."

"But how do you teach about the conquest of Israel?"

Jon could see that the lawyer was attempting to corner him into making a judgment call. "I have never covered that in my classroom, sir. But I have done so in adult Sunday school classes I've taught."

"All right. How about the prehistoric periods?"

"I'm afraid I don't understand the question."

"Do you teach the secular view that man evolved over time from apes, or the religious view that Adam was placed in a garden?"

Jon sighed. He should have been prepared for this. "I use the textbook I am assigned. I use tests that are preprinted. But, yes, I do tell my students that this is only one interpretation of history. I let them know about the alternatives."

"Alternatives? Are there more than one?"

"Well, since we're studying ancient cultures, I usually have related what each of these cultures believed. We usually discuss several creation accounts from cultures around the world."

"So you discuss several *creation* accounts with your students? That's interesting. Why just the cultures who believe in a created world?"

Jon laughed, in spite of his precarious situation. "To my knowledge, sir, there were no other ideas of how the world came to be. Every culture I am aware of includes a higher power of some type in their account of how the world came to be. That is, except our own."

Mr. DeFranco stepped back for a moment and put his head down thoughtfully. He appeared to be considering a new strategy.

"I have a copy of your contract, Mr. Shepherd. The contract you signed with the school board upon being hired by them. Are you aware of the statements it makes regarding such a situation as this?"

"Yes, sir."

"And did you fulfill your contract?"

"I attempted to get permission from my principal to cover the new material."

"Is that what the contract states, Mr. Shepherd? That the principal has the authority to restructure the curriculum content?"

"No, but we have always—"

"No? Well, then. What does it state? For the record."

"I couldn't say exactly." Jon's mind was beginning to cloud.

"Let me read it for you, then. It states: 'All contracted teachers, substitutes, coaches, and staff personnel shall conform in their instruction to the school board rulings on issues pertaining to religion and shall not deviate from the accepted standard without prior authorization from the board.' Were you authorized, Mr. Shepherd—prior to teaching the controversial material?"

"I tried to get permission. I explained that."

"But certainly not on the first day."

"I hadn't taught it yet."

"You testified that you offered your ideas for discussion on both days."

"But I . . ." Jon sensed he was losing the battle. Though desperate to stay ahead of the questioning, the remaining time on the witness stand melted into a blur of accusations.

❧ ❧ ❧ ❧

"Okay, we've got the story about the convenience-store shooting, the water main rupturing downtown, the package bomb in D.C., and that new liposuction method. What's the order here?"

"We need to add an update on the Shepherd trial, too." Watt had not looked up when he made the statement. All eyes turned his direction. Esther dropped her own.

"Branson will give the story. I've written it up myself. It'll be in your scripts for the five o'clock broadcast."

He had thrown his glove into the arena. Esther returned his gaze evenly but groped inwardly for a better response. Why had he rejected her own write-up of the trial? Was it so he could cast a bad light on Jon?

Just minutes before the broadcast was to air, Esther saw her script. Her knees nearly buckled. Watt had written up an interview from an unnamed fellow teacher who made several malicious statements about Jon and his trial. There were allegations of misconduct on his part—entirely unsubstantiated. And Dr. Finley's organization was portrayed as a publicity-seeking front for a fanatical right-wing political group. It was far worse than she had feared. There was no way she could read this on the air.

And then her mind returned to the dismissal of Sybil Horn, her predecessor at the news desk. Had Watt done the same thing to her? Would Esther be the next one to be dismissed?

Throughout the broadcast, as each story passed, Esther

knew the story about Jon was approaching. Still, she was unsure of what to do. There had been no time think. All her quick prayers had seemed to fly meaninglessly away. Now she was approaching the moment of truth.

All too soon, the hateful words began to scroll onto the screen. Esther's breath caught in her throat and choked out her ability to speak. Her vain attempt at mentally editing the script disappeared from her memory. She could remember none of the phrases she had tried to substitute. She was freezing. She was staring blankly at the camera.

Suddenly, she heard a voice beside her. "On the local scene tonight, we have a twist to the now-familiar saga of a young schoolteacher. . . ." It was Steve's voice. Steve was reading the story Watt had written for her. Heart pounding, Esther realized that Steve had placed himself between her and Watt.

As soon as the next break for commercials arrived, Watt came unglued. "Who do you think runs this station? How dare you deviate from the lines you were assigned!"

Esther shot a glance at Steve. For the first time, she saw perspiration across his forehead. He dabbed it away and poised himself to begin again. The remainder of the newscast was a haze. As soon as it was over, Gabe crossed toward Esther and laid a sympathetic hand on her shoulder.

"Branson," Watt's voice crackled from across the room. "O'Neal will be taking your place on the eleven o'clock show. You may go home." And then he added, "Steve Forelli, I will see you in my office immediately."

Her thoughts frozen, Esther moved out of the building and drove home. She could not allow herself to think now. She forced the feelings from her heart. As she approached the front door, it swung open for her.

"Granddad," she whispered. "I think I was fired." Finally, she allowed the tears to flow.

He let her cry, knowing she wasn't ready to answer questions; she needed only his sympathy and comfort first. And, too, he had seen the broadcast. He was quite certain of what had transpired. Patting her hand as she leaned against the kitchen counter, Granddad waited for her to speak.

"I didn't know what to do. I couldn't think. Watt's story was . . . it was so wrong. It was spiteful and mean. None of it was the truth."

"He is a very angry man, Esther."

"I've never seen him use such blatant tactics. He didn't even attempt to write the story based on fact. He didn't even try!"

"He wasn't writing about Jon Shepherd. It had nothing to do with Jon."

Esther looked up with tears still washed across her face. "What do you mean?"

"It was partly an attack on Christianity. But it was much more direct than that, too."

Esther studied his face. "It was me, wasn't it? He did it to hurt me."

"He did it to *beat* you."

"And did he? Did I let Watt win? What could I have done?"

"I don't know, dear. I'm not sure that you could have won. It was *his* game and his rules."

"I couldn't read that story. I couldn't say those things about anyone." But Esther was not quite truthful. "I might have—in the past—when I thought I wasn't responsible for what came out of my mouth on air. I thought I was like a soldier who was just supposed to follow orders. Like it wasn't really me who was accountable. I probably even read awful things like that about someone else, someone I didn't know, and never thought twice."

"Why not tonight, Esther?" He asked the question in a tone that made Esther sure he had been wondering.

"Not because of Jon. Not because I've met him or because of our conversation. Annie asked me some questions yesterday that got me thinking about that very thing. I realized that it's always my responsibility to tell the truth. Not for Jon, but for myself—and most importantly so that I can *pray* without anything standing between me and God. I couldn't possibly risk that again. Not for any job, or any person. It's too much to ask. But I wasn't even kind to Jon. Not really. Steve read the words anyway. Steve saved *me*, but in doing so he crushed Jon. I didn't even accomplish anything. I threw my job away for nothing."

"Jon Shepherd will be glad the words didn't come from you."

"I'm glad." But Esther had another shattering thought. "But Neal . . . Neal will be so upset. And he'll be the first person Watt will call. He'll never forgive me for this."

"Why should you need his forgiveness? You've done nothing wrong."

Esther sank onto a nearby chair before she answered, reaching for a tissue. "I threw away my shot at a great career. That's what Neal will see. And, believe me, that's all that Neal will see."

"And yet you feel he's a good choice for you? Forgive me, Esther, but I cannot keep from expressing how I feel any longer."

"But you've only seen his weaknesses. It's not really fair."

"I know more than you think."

There was more he wanted to say. That much was obvious. Esther was quiet for some time, reluctant to have any more weight laid on her shoulders tonight. Silently she debated with herself about how to respond.

"I'm going to bed, Granddad. I really need to just get some sleep—if I can. Please, can we finish this discussion in the morning?"

"Of course. You should sleep. You're right. It can wait."

Esther turned slowly and trudged toward the stairs. With

a heavy heart she climbed to the top, then turned back. Granddad had not followed her. Esther lowered herself onto the top step and leaned against the spindles. She was tired. Mentally and emotionally exhausted. How could she find the strength to face whatever Granddad had to say about Neal?

"Dear God," she prayed weakly. "I don't know why this is happening. I don't know why you're letting my life—my career . . . my future—just disappear in a single night. Did Watt do this to me? Or was it you? I suppose I shouldn't ask. I'm probably wrong, but if I just knew why, maybe I could figure out what to do. Is that so much to ask?"

Every human fiber of Esther's being begged her to go to her room, to ignore the tugging of her conscience to go back downstairs. She hated the idea. If she already couldn't sleep, how would knowing more awful news make it any easier? Was whatever her imagination could devise between now and the time it took for her to fall asleep more difficult to bear than whatever Granddad had to say?

Finally, Esther rose dutifully and descended the stairs.

# Seventeen

*Wednesday, June 9*

"Esther?" Granddad looked genuinely surprised that she had returned to finish their discussion.

Esther made no attempt to conceal her dismal attitude, dropping onto a chair beside him at the table.

"We can wait to talk until morning," Granddad offered. "Nothing need be said tonight."

"I need to know, Granddad."

He nodded. "I know you had wondered about the connection between your Neal and this Watt Shreve. I believe I have found it."

"Is it bad?" Even with this, Esther spoke the words dispassionately.

"It is." Granddad took a deep breath before proceeding. "I mentioned to you that the name of this Shreve character sounded familiar to me somehow. So as I reacquainted myself with some of my old newspaper contacts, I asked around about him. No one knew much until I spoke with a gentleman in Burlington. He gave me the name of a man who, because he was one of the few who could repair a certain technical doodad, would have visited many stations over the years. You know how it is. You've done this type of work before."

Esther nodded. She was beginning to listen more carefully.

"This man said he had heard of Shreve and that he could remember him as connected to some type of scandal. He was sure it had also been connected to something about religion. That's when I became very concerned. So I tracked down where and when."

"How?"

"I sat in the library searching old microfiche files."

"But how could you have gotten there without my knowing?"

"I had a cab drop me off on my way home from the trial one afternoon. But I didn't find any mention of it there. What I did find were the names of some key employees at the Burlington station who were around while Shreve was there. After that, I just kept calling until someone was willing to talk to me about it. It took a lot of calls."

"What did you find?" Esther's pulse was racing.

"That Watt Shreve is a very bitter man. He hates religion because—well, no, let me back up. You see, Esther, he had a very difficult life. I was able to track down a previous place of residence, and his great-aunt still lives there. She told me that his mother was a very troubled woman. She had no husband and no idea of how to provide a home for her three sons. When Watt was eight or nine, she met a man—another in a long line of men whom she hoped would be the answer to her troubles. This man laid down an ultimatum that he didn't want kids around and she would have to choose him or the boys. In her ignorance, she chose him."

Esther had never even wondered about *why* Watt behaved as he did. "Granddad, that's awful. It's so horrid."

"Watt and his brothers were left at the home of his great-aunt. They were not there long when Watt's older brother ran away. Watt stayed with the younger one. Now, his aunt holds some very strange religious views. She told me on the phone that she is Christian, but also was quite proud to describe how rigidly she raised the boys. Watt and his brother were apparently subjected to harsh discipline and received no love or compassion."

Esther laid her head on her arms against the cool wood of the table. Watt should have received her understanding, not her disgust. But how could knowing any of this really have changed what she had done at work?

"Now, that explains why he had a secret fury toward religious people. The rest of the story is quite simple. While at this previous station, Watt let his pent-up resentment get the better of him and was involved in a conspiracy to bring down a television evangelist. He wasn't the only person out to get this man, but he had the control of a news broadcast, which proved to be a devastating weapon against the minister. In the end, the evangelist was reduced to nothing but stood up to his persecutors and proved that many of the accusations against him were false. He even pursued some of those involved into the court system, but he wasn't able to regain the public trust that the incident had deflated and he never traced the actions back to Watt."

"Then how did *you* find out that Watt was involved?"

"Several of the people I talked to at the station admitted they had known about the whole affair. Once I revealed to them how much information I had already gained, they were willing to give up some of the remaining details. The station had found out about Watt's breach of ethics. They would have turned him in, too, had it not been that the station would have also borne the brunt of the negative public exposure. So they just let him go. Quietly. Very quietly."

Esther's mind was whirling. "Where did he go? To us?"

"Not directly. He had a great deal of difficulty finding a new position where people were satisfied with the unspoken shadow across his resumé."

A large piece of the puzzle fell into place in Esther's mind.

"And that's where Neal comes into the picture."

"I'm afraid so."

"Did he know, then? Did he know the whole story about Watt's dismissal?"

"I'm quite certain he did, Esther. Watt would never have risen back into this level of power if it hadn't been for Neal's hard work on his behalf."

"And, knowing all this, he warned *me*." Esther was no longer speaking to Granddad. She was simply thinking aloud. "He told me to watch what *I* said to Watt. I was his fiancée—yet he chose to ask me to conform so that Watt could be kept out of confrontation. It's no wonder that Watt was calling him to get me back on my leash. Oh, Granddad, I've been such a fool!" Esther's lip trembled now.

"No, child." Granddad was not flinching. Rarely had she seen him so intense and direct. "You have shown yourself to be no one's fool. But it's not over. Watt Shreve will certainly do everything in his power to try to bring down Jon Shepherd. There is no doubt about that."

For what seemed forever, Esther struggled within herself, searching for an answer. "I don't know what to do. I can't stop him. I'm sure I don't even still work at the station." She wanted to flee back upstairs, but she forced her wide eyes up to meet her grandfather's. "What can I do?" she whispered.

His hand reached across the table to grasp hers. "You have to do what you feel led to do. No one can tell you what that is. You have to pray for all you're worth until you know." Leaning in even closer, his eyes locked on her own. "If he can make Jon Shepherd look guilty, he can do it to others, too. If someone doesn't try to stop him, no Christian can feel safe."

"But there's nothing I can do." She was pleading now, wishing with all her heart she could turn away from that intense gaze.

"Esther, dear child, consider this carefully. How do you

know that you weren't put here, in this position, for this very moment?" His voice was clouded with emotion. "God can use you, Esther. I know in my heart that He can use you now—if you're only willing."

His voice softened, almost as if an edge of sadness had crept in. His words came more slowly. "But if you aren't willing, God will move without you. He *will* raise up someone to accomplish His purposes. He always has. Be that person, Esther. Be brave. Be faithful. Be willing to put yourself where God needs you to be."

Esther lowered her face into her grandfather's hands and fought back tears. She was so frightened. She felt so powerless and small. How could he ask so much of her—especially when he couldn't even tell her exactly what it was she needed to do?

Finally, she rose, kissed him, and walked upstairs. Her pulse was racing. Her hands felt clammy as she kneaded them together and leaned onto the desk in her bedroom. What would she do? If she confronted Watt with the new information, she was certain there would not be one person at the station who would stand with her. He would have her fired. Her career would be over. And what if he chose to turn his vengeance on her? She knew that, in his hands, the story of how she lost her job could be turned into an ugly mixture of accusations and deceptions. What would he do to Annie, or to Jon?

And then there was Neal. What would Neal say? They had only just begun speaking again. The wedding date had already been pushed back into obscurity. Well, there was really no question about what he would think. Neal would have nothing to do with her if she broke faith with him in such a direct way, publicly choosing personal convictions over the career that she now understood he had groomed her for from the beginning.

What could she do? How could anything positive come

out of confronting Watt? In desperation, Esther finally began to pray, and once she had begun, everything in her heart poured out. There was no hesitation now to admitting how she felt. There was no stumbling over wording and propriety. Her heart simply burst because it could no longer hold the flood of emotions welling up within it, and for the first time since her conversion, Esther prayed with every part of her being.

❧ ❧ ❧ ❧

Early the next morning, Esther's phone rang. Dreading what she might hear, her voice was strained as she answered.

"What were you thinking?" Annie was clearly not calling to offer sympathy. "Nobody can believe you would be so stubborn. And it's even more incredible that Steve bailed you out. That's way beyond what I can understand. But, anyway, for some strange reason you are still expected to come to work today. Another mystery to me. Watt sure didn't give Sybil a second chance. I guess you've got some kind of guardian angel behind the scenes. That's the only thing that makes sense to me. Maybe Robin really liked you or something."

Esther was dubious. "Is Watt just wanting to fire me in person?"

"No, I think he's really going to let you keep working. But then, Robin comes in a couple days. Maybe Watt's got a plan."

There was nothing left for Esther to do now. She arrived at work and slipped quietly back to her office. How could she express her thanks to Steve? Then again, she was hardly pleased that she had escaped being the one to read the malicious story when it was still aired. She certainly didn't doubt that Steve had been gracious in his actions. Thursday slid slowly by. Esther felt she was hearing the foreboding tick of a time bomb in the office around her. Tomorrow was the day that Robin would arrive at the station. He would not be back again for a month. Esther's mind had been contriving an alarming plan.

Annie had said she had some kind of guardian angel at the station. Annie, who almost always knew what was going on. It couldn't be Neal anymore. She knew him well enough to rule out that likelihood. And none of her co-workers would have the power to help her. In Esther's mind, the only possibility was Robin.

She knew it was a long shot. Robin had only spoken to her on a few occasions, but he had also said that he made it his business to be aware of each member of his staff. He would certainly have known about her refusal on air, and yet he had allowed her to stay. There must have been a reason. He was the only one with the final authority—even over Watt.

As Esther viewed the situation from all angles, she decided she had little to lose. She knew she couldn't go on facing off with Watt each time an issue appeared. Emotionally, if she were going to act at all, it had to happen soon.

She could not confront Watt directly. Not only would it be useless, it would also be what he would expect. Surely, by now he wondered if Esther had an idea about his past. He would be prepared for direct accusation. He would be able to defend himself. And yet Esther knew she would never be able to speak to Robin without Watt being present. There was only one way.

When Esther first told Granddad what she was planning to do, he sat and stared. Then, slowly at first, he began to glow with understanding. "I would never have thought of such an . . . an unusual plan. You're right, Esther. It's a perfect way. It's really the only way. I hope it *works*!"

Esther couldn't help but smile. He was sweet to encourage her so valiantly when what she planned to do must seem to be inane.

"I need to disappear, then," Granddad said.

"What?"

"I can't be here—in your way."

"No, Granddad, I need you to—"

"Without a doubt, I will be supporting you through prayer, my dear girl. But this is something you must do by yourself, without me peering over your shoulder. I will call a taxi to take me to a nearby hotel. I feel strongly, Esther, that I've fulfilled what God intended for me here by probing Watt's past. To do more than what I have done is to meddle. But know this: my prayers for you, and for Jon, will go on continuously."

With tears in her eyes, Esther embraced the man who had led her to God, and who had supported her through one of the most pivotal moments in her life. Had it not been for Andy's death, where would she be right now? What a chain of events that weekend funeral had begun!

# Eighteen

*Friday, June 11*

As morning dawned, Esther rose and began meticulously preparing for work. She chose a cream-colored silk blouse, a royal blue jacket and skirt, and added a designer scarf around the neck as an accent. The shoes and jewelry accents, too, were chosen thoughtfully. Then she began working on her hair and makeup, creating just the right look of softness and style. Her movements were skilled but mechanical. There was no pleasure for her in the appearance of the fashionable young woman whose rigid face stared at her in the mirror.

The drive to work was also a labor, Esther trying hard to repress her deepest emotions, repeating words of prayer for resolve and courage—two things she knew she needed desperately today.

She arrived deliberately early, not being expected until close to three o'clock, but entering the building just after noon—swiping her security badge, walking the long hallway to her office, closing the door, and sinking into her office chair to wait. For Esther, there would be no pretense of working. She would simply wait for Annie to summon her, sitting alone in her office, staring at the door, and trying not to think about what would happen next.

She hadn't wanted to get Annie involved, but she felt her friend had a right to know what she had learned about Watt Shreve and what she was planning to do. So Esther had placed a call long after midnight, explaining it all to the groggy Annie, who was trying to the best of her ability to understand. For once, Annie had not asked a multitude of questions. She seemed to sense the enormity of the task before Esther.

One o'clock flashed onto the clock in Esther's office. Then ten after. Then quarter past. Still Esther waited, her eyes watching the door. Finally, at one-twenty-three, Annie pushed the door open slightly and signaled to Esther that the meeting had begun. Esther rose, trembling and swallowing hard to fight the dryness in her mouth.

Down the long hallway, past the copier room, past the door to the set, and on toward the large meeting room—Robin's meeting room. The station managers would already be assembled there, the meeting almost ready to begin.

Esther did not allow herself to hesitate, afraid that a single pause in her steps would make the courage drain away so that she'd turn and rush back to hide in her office. Instead, she reached up and rapped firmly on the door, then pushed it open.

Looks of astonishment rippled around the room as Esther's eyes swept along the table toward its head. In an instant, she took in the expression on Watt's face. The slight curl of a satisfied smile, the smug expression predicting her downfall, the twinkle of triumph in his eyes. If she had come to accuse, he exuded confidence that he would win. Esther looked past Watt and faced Robin, her stomach lurching with alarm.

Robin sat alertly in his chair, surveying her for an unending moment, his face expressionless and void. Then, with a nod her direction, he asked, "Is there something you'd like to say, Miss Branson?"

This was the time. Esther forced herself to put all thought of anyone else in the room out of her mind and to look only at Robin, to smile and appear charming and confident. She looked deeply into his eyes and stated her purpose as clearly as she could. "I'm so sorry to interrupt your meeting, Mr. Kincaid. But I wanted to invite you to a dinner on Saturday night . . . at my home." There was a breathless pause. "Not a party, just a private dinner. I wanted to invite you, Mr. Kincaid, as well as Mr. Shreve. It would be such an honor if you would come."

There it was. The invitation had been launched across a room full of gaping faces and amazed stares. Even Watt had lost his smug look. This was a step he could never have planned for, nor could he have any idea what would happen next. His face turned over to where Robin was assessing the moment.

Another stretch of silence seemed to last forever. Then the intense look broke into a smile of amusement as Robin seemed to have made his decision concerning Esther's behavior. "I'd like that very much, Miss Branson. I don't get many dinner invitations, especially from someone as beautiful and charming as you." He was accepting her invitation. It was almost unbelievable. "What time would you like me to arrive?"

"May I send a car to pick you up at your hotel at seven?"

He smiled again. "That would be fine."

"Thank you, Mr. Kincaid." She meant the words. Did he have any idea how very much she meant those words? Somehow, she felt he did. As quickly as she had entered, Esther ducked back out of the room, almost unable to maintain her composure until she had closed the door and scurried back down to her office. Annie was already there, pacing back and forth while she waited for Esther to return from her mission.

"What happened? What did he say? Did you ask? Was he angry? Oh, I knew this would never work!"

In a tumbling of emotion, Esther fell into an office chair, choking and sobbing all at once.

"Esther! Esther, did he fire you? What happened?" Annie was frantic for an answer.

"He'll come," Esther gasped. "He'll come."

"He wasn't angry? He said he'd come?" Annie couldn't hide her utter amazement.

"He'll come," Esther repeated, gathering herself together forcefully and wiping away the tears that had formed.

"But why? Why are you crying, then?" Annie was confused, searching Esther's face. "It worked, right? Your plan worked? You got what you wanted?"

With careful words, Esther struggled to make Annie understand. "In a few days I will spend my day cooking for one of the most powerful men in America. And after he comes to my house and eats at my table, I will tell him that the only man at our station with whom he has any real contact at all—his sole source of counsel here—is a cruel bigot. And I will say these things in front of that very man."

Annie gulped down a response.

"Oh, Annie!" Tears threatened again. "What have I done?"

For now, Esther could not think about tomorrow. She knew she had to expel all questions about the dinner from her mind in order to be able to finish her day at the station. There were still meetings to attend and news to read. Somehow she must ignore the rising whispers about her unprecedented interruption of the meeting and continue to perform her tasks for the day.

Only Gabe was direct enough to ask her why she had entered the meeting, but Esther had no idea how to meet his question. She did not dare to answer him truthfully. Instead, she smiled a pleading smile and touched his arm gently before turning and walking away. His doubtful expression followed her as she went.

How could she expect people around her not to make assumptions? She must appear to be insane to them. Or did they think the move was political—a direct attempt at gaining power and position in the station? Esther was certain that all trust she had shared with those around her had been stripped away.

At the anchor desk, Steve was aloof, almost not acknowledging her presence. There were no exchanged glances, no smiles and nods during any of the stories. Esther felt like a puppy with its tail tucked between its legs, whimpering in shame.

Mercifully, the second broadcast finally came to an end and Esther fled to her car to hurry home. She had no energy left to think. She had no emotion left to spill into her tears. She felt cold, passionless, and empty. Her only hope was that she would somehow find the ability to sleep.

❧ ❧ ❧ ❧

"I heard that you're planning a party in my house." It was Neal, phoning her late that night.

Esther scooted up in her bed and turned on the table lamp, noting that Neal's voice held a bitter tone. Obviously, Watt had passed along word of her actions that day.

"Anyway," he continued, "I wanted you to know that you'll need to set another plate. You can bet I'll be there. Whatever career move you're scheming in that mind of yours, I plan to oversee it."

Esther knew her response was feeble, but she could not do better. "I told Mr. Kincaid that it would only be he and Watt."

"They won't mind. Trust me, Esther. Watt'll be glad to see me there."

Esther groaned, but she knew she had no control over

this change of plans. She would be setting four plates for dinner.

"I understand. Good-bye, Neal." Esther's wavering voice threatened to fail her, but she ended the conversation feeling both relieved and frightened. Without question, she knew that chapter in her life had come to a close.

❧ ❧ ❧ ❧

Jon woke suddenly, staring at the dark shadows and pools of eerie light in his room. It was unusual for him to wake in the middle of the night. More unusual still to awake with a clear mind—he who usually had to force his brain into gear with a strong cup of coffee even after a full night's sleep. But now his thoughts came clearly, as if he had not been sleeping at all. Had he heard a sound? He listened carefully to the silence for a clue. There was none.

Instead, he flipped onto his side and crushed his pillow into a better position under his head. It must have been that the pizza he'd had at midnight disagreed with him. Well, he'd just go back to sleep again.

But sleep did not come. Slowly, he became aware of the knot of anxiety in his stomach. He turned onto his back again, running fingers through his hair and staring up through the darkness. He could not imagine what reason he had for suddenly waking and feeling distraught.

Again he tried to find a position in which he could sleep, reaching out beside him to stroke Commodore, who was also awake now. No new position worked. Sleep was evading him. In his mind, there was no good reason for his night to have been interrupted. The trial was progressing, though slowly, and his attorney had assured him that things were moving along well.

Suddenly, Jon became aware of a rising sense of purpose—one totally apart from the court case that usually consumed his thoughts.

Softly, trying not to wake Caleb in the bedroom across from his, he rose and walked to the living room. It was two-thirty in the morning. Taking a seat at his desk, he leaned his head into his hands.

"I don't know what's wrong, Lord. I can't admit to more than a strange feeling that someone is in trouble tonight." The sense was growing stronger as he prayed, the conviction of his words increasing.

"You know, Father. You know who it is. Give them strength. Give them your spirit. Be with them now in their time of need." With more emotion than he understood, Jon prayed for the individual he could not even identify.

# Nineteen

*Saturday, June 12*

Esther's alarm rang at six o'clock sharp on Saturday morning. Immediately she rose to make preparations for the day, first going over her list of food for the evening meal. Annie, again proving herself to be the source of all information pertaining to the people around them, had given Esther a list of restaurants which Robin frequented when he was in town and what his favorite dishes were—all of which she had gleaned from newsroom gossips. It had been a huge relief to Esther to have a starting point in planning the menu.

Before leaving for the grocery store, Esther laid out each serving dish and noted each of the ingredients she would be needing, including a selection of drinks and snack foods. She wanted to be prepared for this evening, no matter what was requested. By this time, it was close to eight o'clock.

First came the stop at the grocery store. Walking through aisles, choosing each item, Esther gathered her ingredients with more care than she had ever thought possible. Loading them into her trunk, she packed the cold foods in the cooler she had placed there. Next, she drove to a local rental shop. Here she was able to find the makings of a perfect table. Wedgwood dishes rimmed in gold. Crystal stemware and fine gold-tone flatware. A stop by the local florist completed her shopping as she purchased several arrangements of cut flowers and various table decorations. She could spare no expense. The dinner had to be perfect in every way.

As soon as she arrived home just after ten o'clock, Esther began cooking. Starting with mixing the bread dough, she moved next to making and filling the pie shells. Soon the house was filled with pleasant aromas. Next, she mixed a marinade for the trout and placed it into the refrigerator while she went on to assemble the individual Beef Wellington pastries for baking. So far, she was right on schedule.

By four o'clock, she had completed all of the preparations she could before the final round of cooking began again. Three pies were cooling on the kitchen table. Cut vegetables to be cooked up later were chilling in a bowl of water in the refrigerator beside the peach soup and marinating zucchini salad. The braided bread and rolls had risen for the last time and were waiting to be popped into the oven for baking.

Next, Esther laid her apron on the counter and moved into the dining room to set and decorate the table. When Neal had purchased the dining room suite, she had no idea they would be using it for the first time in such a frightening way. The centerpiece was positioned and duly fussed over. The candles arranged and the matches laid on the buffet table. Each place setting was given particular attention. Napkins folded just so, flatware and plates perfectly positioned. Stemware waiting to be filled. As she dimmed the light from the chandelier, Esther could see that the dining room was looking just as she had hoped it would.

Now, quickly, she needed to shower and dress. Checking over the list again, she ascended the stairs to the bedroom and kicked off her walking shoes. It was five o'clock. She needed to be dressed and cooking again in about half an hour. Neal had said he would arrive at seven. She was still on schedule. If only nothing happened to ruin her carefully laid plans. Esther could hardly manage the thought without feeling shivers along her spine. And always, in the back of her mind, she knew that the evening, even if everything worked out perfectly, would in all likelihood be the most devastating of her life.

Esther was not aware that Neal had arrived until his voice burst into the silence from directly behind her. "It's incredible," he raved. "The house looks great. The food smells terrific. If I'd known you could pull off this kind of dinner party, I'd have made you do it long ago." Esther was shocked by the swing in his demeanor. Apparently, he had come to assume that Esther's behavior was based solely on ambition. This was something Neal could understand. This was something he respected.

Perhaps, when the evening ended, Neal wouldn't hate her entirely. But no, Esther was certain he would feel utterly betrayed. She wished she could have talked him into staying out of the dinner party.

Hors d'oeuvres had been placed on silver trays in the living room by the time Esther took the main dishes from the oven. Breads were in baskets, keeping warm under linen wraps in the cooled oven. Water glasses were filled, fireplace and candles lit, and soft jazz played in the background. The tension hanging over the house was almost more than Esther could bear. Finally, Neal heralded the arrival of the limousine.

Through the living room window, Esther could see the driver opening the door for Robin. He stepped out onto the curb and strolled up the sidewalk, Watt following behind. Then the doorbell rang. Neal moved gracefully over to answer the door. Esther waited behind him.

"Mr. Kincaid. I was so pleased to hear Esther had invited you for dinner and to hear that you'd accepted. We're so honored to have you in our home."

Robin gave Neal a pondering look then smiled coolly as

if he had already lost interest in the unexpected guest.

"Good evening, Mr. Kincaid," Esther offered, gathering her courage and extending her hand. "I'd like to introduce you to Neal Parker."

"Good evening, Miss Branson. Mr. Parker."

"Please, come in." As Robin passed into the living room, Esther was certain that out of the corner of her eye, she saw Neal and Watt exchange satisfied glances.

"You have a lovely home, Miss Branson."

"Please, call me Esther."

Robin turned and smiled fully at her. His white hair shimmered in the flickering light of the candles. His blue eyes shone, and Esther realized, for the first time, that Robin knew she had not invited him simply for a pleasurable evening. He knew there were ulterior motives behind it, and he seemed somehow amused at the game they were playing.

She smiled in return. If she weren't so terrified of him, Esther could almost believe she would enjoy his company.

"May I get you a drink?" Neal stepped forward to ask as soon as Robin had selected a chair. Watt followed suit and for a short time the men chatted together, as if they were friends, each feigning common interests with Robin.

After several minutes had passed, Esther left the living room to gather the remaining dishes and set them on the buffet hutch. The bowls of chilled peach soup she set on each dinner plate. With a last look at the table settings, she strode to the living room and waited for a break in the conversation so she could invite them to the table.

Once again, seated around the dinner table, conversation was trite and shallow. Neal and Watt seemed to have plenty to say, but Robin chose his words thoughtfully. Esther, too, said little but smiled often—glad to have the activity of playing hostess to give her reasons to speak infrequently but still have something with which to busy herself. She was biding her time, hoping to inadvertently reveal nothing of her intentions.

"I can see that the show is going well," Neal prompted Watt to boast for them all.

"Yes. Our ratings are soaring. We've never had so many sponsors knocking at the door. We've developed a very good lineup of reporters, and our anchors are the best in the business." Watt grinned at Esther. She returned a forced smile.

Esther allowed the conversation to linger, her mind spinning. The pies had been served. Now they were scraping the last of the filling and crumbs from their plates. Esther's mind was whirling. How should she begin her discussion? And when?

Then Robin spoke. "I sensed a little trouble on the set last Wednesday."

The sentence hung in the air. Watt shrank back from it, clearly surprised. Esther forced her lips to speak. There would not be a better chance.

"It was my fault. Steve Forelli tried his best to cover up for me. He was so generous to do that, but it was my doing."

Robin's eyes fell on her, waiting for the explanation to follow.

"Mr. Kincaid," she tried to keep the pleading tone from creeping into her voice. "The news segment I was unable to read on air was in regard to Jon Shepherd. I told you once—on the day you were deciding whether or not to offer me the co-anchor position—that I make it my responsibility to understand the whole scope of each issue. In this story especially, I do understand what is going on." She looked down in an effort to gather courage together. Watt was hanging on every word, half aware of what she might say next. Neal eyed her suspiciously.

"The story I was given to read was untrue. It was filled with deliberate insinuation and . . . well . . . and lies."

There were gasps of disbelief coming from the far end of

the table. Esther did not look in their direction. She was watching Robin's unflinching face, forcing herself to continue.

Suddenly, she no longer cared about the result. She was certain she was doing the right thing, that tonight she would sleep in peace. Her heart grew bolder as she continued. "Mr. Shreve wrote the story, completely disregarding the piece I had already researched and written. He did so with malice toward Jon Shepherd, discrediting him in every way possible, Mr. Kincaid.

"I have been given proof from a very reliable source that this is not Mr. Shreve's first attempt to slander men in positions of authority who are Christians, and each situation has been thoroughly verified. At our station there were the stories about the East Marbrey Christian Church, where Mr. Shreve's script slandered the deacon's son, and the more recent attempt to implicate Stephen Josephson as being part of the laundering of public funds. In neither case were there any grounds to accuse these people of wrongdoing. But both shared a common thread. Both of these men who were maligned were Christians."

Stopping only for a breath, Esther continued. "My source has given me some other indisputable evidence. Mr. Shreve was released from a news director position in Arkansas because it was proven that he deliberately slandered a television preacher.

"Once his actions had been revealed to those he worked under, he was released from employment. But the station kept the proceedings private in order to protect their own reputation. They were too concerned about ratings.

"Mr. Shreve has now set his sights on Jon Shepherd. I'm afraid of what he might do to further malign Jon's character and further threaten the reputation of this station." Esther's eyes had not left Robin's face as she spoke the words.

There was a painful moment of silence. Then Robin rose.

"I am going to need an opportunity to think through all of the things that you've just told me, Miss Branson." His eyes were darkening, but he was guarding his composure carefully. "Please excuse me for a moment." Esther nodded an unblinking response.

Robin walked out onto the back porch, leaving Esther alone with Watt and Neal.

"Are you crazy, Esther?" Neal shrieked as quietly as he was able.

"Shut up," Watt shot back. "Do you want him to hear you?"

Neal turned his face toward Watt. "And what are *you* thinking? You said you were going to watch your step this time."

Watt rose quickly and moved toward Esther. "Who told you? Who was your source?"

Then Neal came to stand between Esther and Watt, not so much to protect Esther as to get the answers to his own questions. "Is it true? Are you going after someone else? Didn't you learn anything from last time?"

"You said she'd buckle. You said we could control her. Is she under control, Parker? Have you handled her?"

"That's not my fault. When you gave her that job I *could* get her to do what I wanted. You pushed her too far."

Watt turned his rage on Esther. "Don't think I can't still break you, Branson. I'm not out yet."

"You are both fools." Robin had reentered the room. He walked slowly around the table to where the other men stood. "You choose to be involved in illegal activities that could very well have my station's license revoked, and then you add to that a threat against the only person in this room who remains in my employ."

Watt winced at Robin's strong words. His eyes darted from person to person in the room, anxiously searching for help to come from somewhere. Finally, he pushed past Neal and fled from the house into the gathering darkness.

Neal looked slowly from Esther to Robin, then back to Esther. Quietly, he also turned and walked out of the house. They heard his car start, then speed away. Silence followed.

"You give an interesting dinner party, Miss Branson."

Esther watched his face as he spoke. She was amazed at how composed he had managed to remain through the whole ordeal.

"If there had been any other way," she urged, hoping he would understand. "If I could have found any other way . . ." The words hung unspoken.

He smiled in return. "You chose wisely. No one could have been more clever in the way you made your findings known." He added, as if confiding in her, "We're lucky to have you—and this Jon Shepherd is fortunate because of your acquaintance, as well. Your courage has very likely saved him from much trouble."

"I'm afraid that courage is something I'm only beginning to understand, Mr. Kincaid. And, I must say, I didn't do it just for Jon Shepherd. I did it because I knew it was the right thing to do."

"I respect you for that." Robin excused himself to head for the waiting limousine and Esther watched him go, the taillights reflecting on the pavement. Then she turned and surveyed the work for her to do in her dining room. *No, that isn't really true. This is Neal's dining room, and I'll soon be leaving his home.*

With a sigh, Esther began to gather the dishes.

❧ ❧ ❧ ❧

Sunday was a day of great celebration for Esther and her granddad. His eyes had shone brightly through all of Esther's telling of the day. He was more than proud of her. He was overjoyed—especially because of the happy ending.

But it was with deep disappointment that Esther accepted his decision to return to Nebraska. She had suspected that he might need to be leaving soon but had chosen to put the thought out of her mind. His *short trip* had stretched to a month and they both knew it must come to an end.

"Do you think you'll be able to visit again soon?"

"It would be nice, dear. I'm afraid I can make no promises, though."

"I'll miss you." Esther could feel her eyes filling with tears.

Granddad's own eyes were misting over. "There's no reason we can't call each other often. And we'll be together at Christmas, surely."

"I will *definitely* come back home for Christmas."

He paused to consider how to phrase what was in his heart. "I'm so grateful I could be with you at this time in your life, Esther. Partly because I like to think I was some encouragement to you, and partly because I've been very personally encouraged that I could still be involved in something important. I cannot tell you how much energy it has given me to be involved again in the news world—going after the *scoop* behind the scenes. How I've missed my old friends and exciting life! But I think I am mostly glad to have been here because I feel so honored to have watched my granddaughter behave in such a courageous and upright way. I shall never forget your struggle and your determination to rise above it no matter what it cost."

There were no words to respond with. Esther let her tears fall. Could she have even taken the stand if Granddad had not been with her? God must have known she would need him. Without a doubt, God had provided everything she had needed.

❧ ❧ ❧ ❧

At ten o'clock on Monday, Esther slipped into the back row of the courtroom seating. At this time, they were deeply involved in the testimony of a geologist who was attempting to serve as an unbiased expert to decide whether the theories proposed by Dr. Finley in his book were compatible with what he had observed around the world. It was apparent that this man had not previously been exposed to some of the information.

For two more grueling hours, he frowned in deep thought, then answered to the best of his ability whether or not he felt that the theory was in compliance with the facts presented. Esther tried to understand, to listen carefully, point by point, and concentrate on the dizzying array of scientific terminology and technical descriptions.

Finally, the judge had mercy and called a recess for lunch. Esther retreated into the foyer and tried to stretch inconspicuously.

"Hi there," she heard Jon's voice behind her. "It's good to see you here, as ever. But I noticed your grandfather is missing. There's nothing wrong, I hope."

"Granddad headed home this morning." Esther knew she had offered an abbreviated answer, that the concerned expression on his face really deserved more information, but she was still fighting her own sadness and could not trust her voice with any more information.

Jon seemed to understand what she couldn't say. "I'm sure you'll miss him." He chuckled a little. "*I'll* miss him. He's a very special person. I was always so encouraged to see him out there watching the trial."

Esther smiled. "He'll be a hard act to follow, but I'll do my best."

"Well, he wouldn't have enjoyed today. It's pretty dry." There was an awkward pause. "Hey, can I buy you a soda?" He motioned to the hallway near the telephones, where they had first met.

Esther watched from behind as he reached into his pocket for more change. She was fighting the urge to fix his collar, which wasn't quite tucked properly beneath his jacket at the back. "How do you think the morning went?"

Jon sighed and turned to face her. "I can't tell. First, I think we're making so much sense that the jury has to see it. Then I think our whole argument is falling apart in front of their eyes. And we've spent so much time on the details of the theory I think we've lost sight of what the real issue is. Sometimes I wonder if this whole case wasn't pretty much decided before we were even sworn in."

"It was." Esther was trying hard not to sound pious, but she really wanted to help Jon see the big picture again. "Remember, you said yourself that God was the one in control, not you. I guess, then, that the lawyers and the jury really don't have control, either. So this case *was* decided long ago."

He nodded silently, letting her words sink in.

"Well, I do have some news that I'm hoping will be good."

"I could use some good news. What is it?"

Esther popped open her soda before answering, letting the suspense build. "I spoke with the owner of our station. He's going to let me do a series of taped interviews with you. He wants to meet you first, just to make sure you're not a nut. But then, if you have time—and if you're still interested—we can continue spending some time discussing the case together, on and off camera." Esther tipped the can to her lips, enjoying having the upper hand while Jon stood dumbfounded.

As quickly as he could, Jon struggled to catch up. "You mean, after the story that aired last week, your station wants to give me a chance to tell this from my viewpoint? Why? What's the catch? Why the sudden interest in giving me a fair shake?"

This was the question Esther wasn't sure she could answer yet. "That's a really long, long story. But mostly, I asked that your trial be covered honestly. I want you to have a few moments in the spotlight to say what's on your heart. You have a good heart, Jon. People need to be able to see it. It makes them understand the issue for what it really is, and not what the media sharks are trying to make it so that the story sells better."

"But why? Why does your station want to throw away the better story to go after the one behind it? I don't understand the sudden change."

Esther looked away, wishing she could put into words all that had happened. "Well, our news director was fired on Saturday. That's a big change." She struggled for a moment to explain more but found that words failed her.

"And you? It sounds like you're in the middle of this somehow. Are you okay?"

"I will be." Esther tried to say it with confidence. Visions of the questioning eyes around her at work and of the angry faces of Neal and Watt flashed across her mind.

For a moment they stood together in silence. Then Jon spoke. "I'd like to do the interviews. I'd like to have a chance to tell my side—and I'd like to see more of you."

"You mean, without people pushing past to use the phone or get a soda?"

He smiled. "Yes. I'd like that."

"Maybe we can find some time tomorrow. Give me a call. And, Jon, good luck this afternoon."

"Thanks."

When Esther entered the office again later that day, she got very mixed reactions. General information had been passed around that Watt had been fired over the weekend and that somehow Esther had a pivotal role in the situation. Most of the workforce had already heard about the private dinner party. Coupled with Watt's immediate dismissal, Esther had become somewhat frightening in the eyes of most of her co-workers. She could see they were wondering what type of power she wielded, able to pull down the most powerful person at the station.

To her great relief, Esther found that her co-anchor was still speaking to her. Steve did not mention the previous days but simply picked up again as if nothing had happened. She had not realized until now how much the wall between them had upset her.

Gabe, on the other hand, took the first moment he could to throw an arm around Esther's shoulder and tell her that even though he didn't have a clue what had gone on, he was glad to be able to still be working together. "I've always liked you, Esther." Then he added with a deep laugh, "But I've never liked that Shreve character. If it was a matter of choosing between the two of you, we sure did keep the right one."

Somehow, the plan had succeeded far beyond Esther's wishes. With all her heart, she repeated a prayer of thanks as she drove away from the station that night.

❧ ❧ ❧ ❧

The first time Esther and Jon could find to meet came on Saturday. Because the weather was nice and they had both been spending so much time indoors, he suggested that they meet at a park near his home. Esther readily agreed. She would much rather walk than sit.

From their first moment together, Esther felt that meeting to talk with Jon was like a fresh breeze in her life. Laughter came easily and often between them, whether they were focusing on interview questions or just chatting.

In fact, the interview format provided the perfect opportunity for Esther to ask all of the questions she would have wanted to know about him had they just been acquaintances. She learned about his upbringing in Germany; how the experience of his growing up overseas had created in him a world view entirely different from what he saw displayed in the American friends he had made once his family moved back to the United States. Jon had been fourteen when his father's health had begun to fail and they moved to Wisconsin where his father became a pastor in a quiet rural church.

She listened while he described in rich detail the periodic passes his family had made through European countries and, eventually, to the Holy Lands. Esther watched his animated face as he described historical sites that she had never really thought of as being real. It was obvious that these trips were what had sparked in him an insatiable interest in history.

And, as they later toured the youth center together, Esther watched his eyes light with a fire of compassion when he spoke about the poverty and despair he had seen here in his homeland—not only in the inner city, but reflected in the cultural poverty of the suburbs as well.

It was beginning to come together for Esther—who he was and what had motivated him to take his stand in court. Every moment of his life, Jon had been prepared for this. What else could he have done but teach? Where could he be but with the young people whom he felt most needed to hear him offer better solutions to their problems? And that was why, when opportunity arose to offer what Jon considered to be an avenue of hope to his students, he had been quick to take a stand. He had truly hoped that there would be at least one student in the infamous science class whose heart was ready to hear, perhaps for the first time, that his entire existence had not been by chance and accident. That he had been designed: soul, body, and mind.

Sunday dawned and Esther dressed carefully, choosing a pastel sundress for another day with Jon. Before leaving him the previous afternoon, he had invited her to attend his church service with him. She had been delighted to accept, and they had agreed to meet in the foyer a few minutes before the service was scheduled to begin.

It was a "modern" church, in Granddad's words, with a rhythm section playing choruses and an easygoing format. But suddenly, sitting with Jon, she felt at home with it. The people were friendly and warm. The smiles genuine and wide. And Esther could clearly see how much they treasured Jon Shepherd.

Later that day, over Sunday dinner with Jon and Caleb, Esther listened as they described their family: their mother, Cynthia, who was lively and full of joy; their father, Mark, who was thoughtful and intense, much like Jon himself; and the youngest brother, Boyd, who was currently training to be a veterinarian. It was obvious that they loved and admired one another.

"Caleb, how did you come to be adopted into this family?" Esther asked, caught up in the conversation now for her own interest's sake, and not for the story she would write.

"I was seven and Boyd was five when our parents were killed in a car accident. We had a little sister, too, but she was in the car with them." Caleb spoke about it easily, as if he had truly come to accept the loss, one far more devastating than Esther could imagine. She thought now about how the loss of her own father had almost destroyed her relationship with her mother.

"We really didn't have anyone to stay with. Mom and Dad—I mean, the Shepherds—were pastoring the church in town, and he was serving as chaplain for the county police department. So they got this call in the middle of the night to see if they would take care of us—temporarily."

"We're still looking for someone who will take them in. Nobody's interested." Jon grinned playfully. Caleb rolled his eyes. Apparently this was a long-standing joke.

"Now, let me get this straight. This was in 1982, and that would make you about sixteen, Jon?" Esther probed in true journalistic fashion.

"Well, fifteen, actually. They came in July. My birthday is late September."

Esther could not avoid the obvious question. "How difficult of an adjustment was it to suddenly have two younger boys in the house?"

"I guess it could have been tough. Mom and Dad were just very careful to give me my space—not lay too much responsibility on my shoulders—and create times when we could all enjoy one another's company. You need to remember, though, I got a driver's license that fall. I don't remember hanging around home an awful lot. I had a job. I had friends to visit and youth group meetings and basketball. Mom was the one who really worked to see that they were taken care of. And Dad was able to help a lot because his schedule was a little more flexible than a typical nine to five."

"How did it feel for you, Caleb?"

The younger brother seemed almost surprised by the question directed at him. He paused for a moment to reflect, clearly trying to respond as honestly as possible. "Really awkward, for a while. It's funny. I guess the biggest problem I had in adjusting to the new family was that *I* was supposed to be the big brother. Boyd had always thought of me as the oldest, the one he looked up to. Now here was this guy—almost an adult in my eyes—making Boyd think that the sun and moon rose and fell around him."

Jon's brow furrowed in wonder. "I didn't know you felt like that."

"You remember how he used to always ask you to drive him to the mall? He loved it when you'd take him places. How could I compete with that?"

Esther looked from one brother to the other. "So what happened? What made you feel better about the situation?"

"He left." Caleb's answer was short but frank. "It's not that I didn't like Jon. In my eyes, even then, he was just so cool. But gradually he wasn't around nearly as much, and I felt like I had Boyd back. I had lost everyone else in my family, and I missed them terribly, especially at first. There was something about sharing Boyd that made it harder to take. Then, after we were legally adopted a couple years later, I didn't feel like Jon was my competition anymore. I felt I had a place in the family again, and that I wasn't just borrowing Jon's."

Jon was still shaking his head in amazement. "That's bizarre. I can't believe you never told me that before." Then he laughed aloud. "So when did you become *my* big brother?"

Caleb was turning red but asked, "What do you mean?"

"You clean my house. You try to tell me what to wear—and not to wear. You bug me about keeping my checkbook balanced and the oil changed in my car. You're either my big brother or a really ugly wife."

Caleb was laughing, too. "Yeah, well, one of these days you're *going* to get married. Then I can have my own life back." Caleb was grinning at Jon meaningfully, who was refusing to look up and meet his eye. Esther was sure she saw his face blush sheepishly. Only a moment passed before he recovered and changed the subject.

All too soon, Esther had to excuse herself. She had already stayed much longer than intended. Jon walked her to her car.

"Thanks, Jon, for a terrific day. I have really enjoyed getting to know you and Caleb better."

"I'm glad you could join us. I know Caleb really enjoyed talking with you, too." He smiled, and his eyes seemed to hold something more, something hidden.

"I guess I'll see you Tuesday, then, for taping."

"I guess so. Promise not to make me look like a dumb clod?"

Esther laughed and pulled her car door closed.

It was eleven-thirty before Esther reached Annie's house, but she knew her friend would be waiting. She had not mentioned any of the plans for her evening to Jon. She hadn't really disclosed much of her own life to him—had not mentioned Neal or their broken engagement or the trouble at the station. She had spent the evening boxing up her possessions and tonight she would be moving them to Annie's home.

The duplex was going to be very crowded, and Esther had hated to admit that there was no other short-term answer to her need of a place to stay. Annie had been adamant, however, and would have moved Esther's belongings on her own had Esther ever allowed her to have a key for the big house.

There was not even the least attempt on Annie's part to hide her relief that Esther's engagement with Neal had ended. She had never made any secret of her dislike for the man. And now Esther realized that, once again, Annie's ability to judge character was much more trustworthy than her own. But, try as she did, she could not force the two pictures of Neal to come together in her mind. She knew he had turned out to be unethical and manipulative, but she would miss him anyway. There were so many memories of happy and touching times spent together. Esther knew that in the coming days she would grieve silently at losing him.

# Twenty

*Tuesday, June 22*

Court was not in session on Tuesday, so Esther had planned to use the morning to get some of her interviews with Jon on videotape. In her mind she had orchestrated how the interview would look on camera. First, she would show Jon walking into the youth center. There would be shots of him coaching, talking with other workers and kids, and teaching one of the job skills classes that the center offered. During all of this, Esther would narrate an introduction to the man, the Jon Shepherd she wanted the viewing audience to see. Then she would cut to a personal interview at the station. She had great hopes for how the piece would turn out.

They planned to tape all morning, first at the youth center and then on a makeshift set that Esther had requested be assembled in a corner of the broadcast room. She had selected a backdrop earlier that morning, then arranged two comfortable chairs, a coffee table, several plants, and a decorative bookshelf toward the back. All this had been set in place and was waiting when she and Jon arrived back from the center.

"Wow. This is incredible. I've never been on a TV set before. It's smaller than I pictured it. And there are a lot more cables and things. How do you even move around in here?"

"You get used to it," Esther chuckled. "We'll be over here. Did you bring other clothes to change into?"

"Yeah. I've got them in my garment bag. Do you want me to change now?"

"Yes, please. There's a dressing room there at the back. I'll have the cameras moved into position while we wait for you."

It wasn't long until Jon returned, dressed in a sport coat and tie. Esther was also ready, and the cameramen were present. "If you can have a seat over there, Jon, Marissa is going to check your hair and fix you up with just a little makeup."

"Makeup? I didn't realize that would be included in the deal. We didn't do that at the center."

Esther had forgotten that Jon was not familiar with all the particulars of a television interview. "We weren't shooting close-ups then or using special lighting. Do you mind?"

"No, not really. I just didn't expect it."

"Sorry, I should have told you."

"Any more surprises on the way?"

Esther laughed and turned to take her place on the makeshift set for a sound check. They were almost ready to begin.

After explaining to Jon that any amount of editing was possible during this type of interview and that he could stop and rephrase any answer that he liked, she began. First the easy questions, and then into the more personal elements of his life and convictions. Esther was amazed at how articulate Jon was. There were few questions that required more than one attempt at his answering.

It seemed like no time before she had gathered all the footage she felt she needed and was taping her own summary statements and her thanks to Jon on air for his openness and cooperation. She concluded with wishing him a successful and speedy trial.

"That's it?" The taping had gone quickly for Jon as well. "We're done?"

"For today. I don't think we'll need any more, but until I do some editing on this, I won't know for sure. How do *you* think it went?"

Jon leaned back into his chair and let out a deep breath. "I don't have any idea. What do you think?"

"I think it was a very good interview. I think you'll come across very well on camera, and there's no question in my mind that you represented yourself well. You should consider a job in television."

"The way I'm sweating under these lights and in this makeup, I think I'll stick with what I've got."

True to his word, Jon hurried back to the dressing room to wash off the makeup and change back into his casual clothes. By the time he returned, Annie had shown up and was chatting with Esther. He strode across the room to where they were, stepping carefully around the cables and other equipment.

"Annie, I'd like to introduce you to Jon Shepherd. Jon, this is Annie Saunders. She works in our tape room, but we're also old friends. We roomed together in college."

"It's nice to meet you, Annie. How did you both end up working here?"

"Oh, Neal finagled a job for Esther, then Esther did the same for me."

Esther blushed. She still hadn't mentioned anything about Neal to Jon, and she certainly didn't like the way that comment sounded. "Well, I think we're done in here. Do you have plans this afternoon, Jon?"

"No, since the trial doesn't resume until tomorrow, I'm a free man today—so to speak."

"I'm sure that's a relief."

"Actually, Esther, I was wondering if I might be able to treat you for lunch? I know you're busy. But I'd sure like it if you have a little time to spare." He was looking boyish again. Esther tried not to notice.

"You don't know the system here. Usually the interviewer treats the 'interviewee' out of gratitude for all the time and work it took to get the interview done."

"Let's buck the system. It'll be my pleasure to treat you."

A mischievous grin was spreading over Annie's face. Esther was grateful she was holding her tongue, but she knew Annie well enough not to expect silence for long.

"Okay. I've got an hour or two before I'm due back. Let's go."

Jon turned to lead the way through the jungle of equipment. Annie marched along on Esther's heels.

"He's cute, Esther," she sang into her friend's ear. Esther swung her elbow back just a little and ignored the remark.

Lunch together was filled with pleasant conversation. It felt as if they had known each other for a very long time, and as Esther watched Jon speak openly and comfortably about any topic they happened to discuss, it made her realize just how closed and guarded Neal had always been. The comparison itself bothered her. With the imprint of her missing engagement ring still on her finger, Esther was not looking to begin a new relationship now. Yet she couldn't help feeling drawn to Jon.

"I can't believe how many ways people find to make generalizations and judgments about other people." Jon was leaning onto the table and twisting the paper from his straw. "You study history at all and you can't help seeing the pattern. Whether it's a difference of religious beliefs or which clothes to wear. It just seems like we keep falling into the same traps of setting up social structures that divide us into little groups and cliques, instead of seeing people as individuals with a God-given right to make choices. Then one group or another starts to try to take the upper hand and force everybody to think the way they do."

Esther was nodding, watching his face carefully as he spoke.

"It's the same thing again with my trial. Parents didn't want their kids to hear what I had to say because it hadn't been 'approved by the board.' You think that we live in an age of openness and acceptance of diversity, and then you go to court because you referred to the Bible in school. They can talk about abortion issues and homosexuality and violence of all kinds, but I can't talk about God. I don't think that's progress. I think all we've accomplished in the last few decades is to exchange the over-Christianized morality people fought against during the sixties for another set of restrictions—this 'political correctness'—about what can and can't be discussed. That's just not progress. It's as if, somehow, we're still afraid of a free exchange of ideas."

"Do other teachers have the same problem? Have you heard them say they feel like their lessons are 'edited for content'?"

"Sure. Some of them fall in line and only say what's been approved. Some of them just go for broke, say what they want to say, and wait to see if they get busted for it. I know one lady, bless her heart, who saves it all up for the last day of classes and then gives a brief testimony to her kids about what she believes as a Christian. She doesn't preach at them. She doesn't put pressure on them one way or the other. I agree we can't have that. I'm just saying we've got to allow for an honest sharing of different kinds of beliefs and opinions."

Esther nodded again, contemplating the dilemma Jon faced.

"And since I started this whole trial thing, I've met so many Christians who actually believe that the solution is to silence anybody who disagrees about God creating the world. That's not what the Bible models, either. Jesus could have shut down all of the false doctrines and the differences of belief. But He didn't. What He did was demonstrate a better way."

Esther was drifting deeper into thought. "I guess if God

had intended to strip us of our freedom to think for ourselves, He wouldn't have planted the tree in the garden in the first place. Allowing us the ability to choose what we believe is what cost God His own Son. Could it be more clear just how important our freedom was to God?"

Jon was openly staring at her now, leaning closer in amazement. "You're right. That's a perfect way to put it." He leaned back again and smiled. "You'd have made a good teacher, Miss Branson. You explain yourself well."

"Not me." Esther turned away and shook her head playfully. "That occupation is too high risk—too much stress for my blood. I'll stick with live television any day."

It was the first time Esther had heard Jon laugh heartily, really throw his head back and belly laugh. She liked it. It was contagious, and she hoped they'd have plenty more opportunities to laugh together. Despite her best efforts to avoid her feelings, Esther was realizing that she was becoming very drawn to this Jon Shepherd.

Once the trial began again, Esther saw very little of him, except for the brief recesses during the morning sessions. She continued to show up at the courtroom, sitting in the back row and struggling to keep up with the scientific lingo. She missed Granddad desperately now that he had returned home. It had been so much more comfortable to be seated with him in the courtroom.

In the afternoons, when Jon was free, Esther was at work. He saw her only on the small television in his living room, but he had become a faithful viewer of the evening news, often watching both the six and eleven o'clock broadcasts.

By the time Friday arrived, Esther was beginning to face the fact that she would need to be candid with Jon about her recent past if she intended to let their relationship progress any further. When she listened to a message he had left on her answering machine Friday night inviting her to get together with him on Saturday, she knew it was time to give him all the difficult details, no matter how awkward she felt about doing so.

They met at a shopping mall and walked from store to store for a while, chatting about insignificant things. Then Esther broached the issue, as cautiously as she could.

"I never really told you the long version about how my station changed its slant on your story. Are you still interested?"

"Of course. I've wondered about that several times since we talked. I was hoping you'd bring it up again when you were ready."

Esther walked over to the second-floor railing, looking down at the food court below. Leaning against the rail, it seemed easier to avoid making eye contact with Jon.

"I guess it sounds a little like fiction now. Our news director was—well, a zealous bigot. He was doing the best he could to use his position to persecute religious people whenever he had opportunity in the news. He did have a difficult upbringing, but of course that doesn't excuse him. It just makes me sorry for him."

Esther was amazed she had even been able to summarize the information so quickly. Now that a little time had passed, it was almost impossible to believe it was real. She looked over at Jon, who was doing his best to absorb what she had said.

"How was he exposed?" Jon asked.

"That's a story, too. You knew that my granddad used to be in the newspaper business. He heard me mention Watt's name and thought he had heard it before. He didn't think he recollected the name with fondness, either. Well, he did some digging around and called some old friends." Esther smiled. "He's an amazing man. As it turned out, he was right. Watt had been involved in a pretty serious situation at a previous station where he broadcast lies about an evangelist."

"You're kidding!"

"I wish I were." Esther took another deep breath. "So, anyway, Watt was dismissed from that station as soon as they found out about his involvement, but the whole thing was kept private because it wouldn't have been good publicity for the station, either. When he was hired at our station several years ago, nobody knew any of that. There hadn't been anyone who was willing or able to reveal the details."

"How did it all come out?"

Esther tipped her head back and looked up at the skylights for a moment. How could she explain it? "Granddad told me. And I told Robin Kincaid, the station's owner. I had no idea if he'd believe me or not, but I couldn't live with myself if I didn't try to pass along what I knew."

"That's incredible, Esther. You must have been terrified it would blow up in your face."

"Believe me, I was!" With all of her being, Esther wanted to end her story there, but she knew that Jon deserved to hear the rest. "My job wasn't the only thing I was risking. You see, I was engaged at the time. And I had just learned that Watt and my fiancé, Neal, knew each other. Neal was the one who got Watt a job at our station. Then later Neal used that previous acquaintance with Watt to get me a job, too. And later still, it was Neal who pushed Watt to give me a chance at the co-anchor position."

Jon was very quiet now, apparently sifting through each word Esther had said.

"I had no idea they knew each other," Esther continued. "And I had absolutely no idea that there was any reason for my promotion except my own performance. It's not hard to believe now, looking back, but I was very naïve and didn't really suspect a thing."

For some time, they looked out in silence over the shifting crowds below them. Finally, Jon spoke. "It must have hurt you very deeply to find out something like that about someone you loved. I'm so sorry."

"Annie says I should have seen all the signs. She thinks that from the start Neal looked at me as someone he could promote and that he was interested in me for that reason alone. I'm not sure I believe her. I mean, it fits all the things that happened between us, but I still don't like to think he was quite that conniving. I think he was just highly ambitious and that his morals were lacking. That's a dangerous combination, but I don't think even he understood that he was making choices to compromise other people and himself. And he was never mean to me, never pushed me into things I wasn't ready for. It was really amazing that he put up with my Puritan ethics for as long as he did. I think he did love me, in his own way.

"And," Esther continued soberly, "I wasn't the person I should have been, either. I'd been raised in a Christian home and community, but I never really made a personal commitment to God until this spring. Maybe if I'd been living the way I should have been, I would have been able to see the problems in my relationship with Neal long before any of this happened. I'll never know what might have been different, but I do think I share some of the blame. And I'm so grateful that God kept me safe through all of it. I just keep thinking about what might have become of me without His hand of protection."

Jon was still silent, seeming to absorb all that Esther had said. After waiting for some time for him to respond, Esther tried to continue. "I hope you don't think I was withholding any of this from you. It's strange to be explaining it, even now. Maybe I'm dumping too much on you. I . . . I hope you're not overwhelmed."

Jon shook himself out of his deep thoughts. "No. No, I'm glad you did. I'm sure it wasn't easy, and I respect you for being so honest." After another long pause, he pushed himself away from the railing and forced a smile. "How about some frozen yogurt?"

"Okay." Esther turned and finally allowed herself to meet his gaze.

"Come on. I'll treat." He winked down at her. Esther could not have been more grateful to change the subject.

The remainder of the afternoon together was pleasant, free from any more difficult discussions. After walking the loop around another level of the shopping mall, they decided to head to the basement and try some bowling. It had been years since Esther had been bowling, and Jon was not above letting her know how much it showed.

When they finally admitted that they each had other places they needed to be, Jon walked Esther out to her car in the parking garage and stood beside it while she unlocked the door and climbed inside. She rolled down her window so they could finish saying good-bye.

"Are you going to church anywhere tomorrow?"

"I *was* attending not far from my house, but I'm staying with Annie in another section of the city now. It seems silly to drive all the way back there. I didn't really get a chance to know people well, anyway."

"Would you like to come to my church again?"

"Do you mind?"

"No. I'd really like to see you there—and I know Caleb would like to see you again, too."

"Well, I guess I will. Thanks."

"Good. I'll see ya." Jon's smile was soft and sincere, filling Esther with warmth. She returned his smile, her heart welling with gratitude.

"Good-bye," she whispered in return. Backing out of her parking spot and driving away, Esther caught sight of him in her rearview mirror, offering a little wave in her direction before turning away.

# Twenty-one

*Monday, July 12*

Esther was amazed at the tension she felt around her during closing arguments of the trial. The longer the trial had progressed, the more crowded the small courtroom had become—and the more frequent the "calls to order" from the judge. At times, he had been forced to rap loudly with his gavel to get the room back under control. Esther could not help but notice how troubled Jon became each time feelings escalated.

Now things were drawing to a close for Jon. Each lawyer was having his final chance to plead his side to the jury members. Esther tried to gauge how much their heads bobbed as each man spoke, but she was unable to convince herself that she could foresee the outcome. It would be close.

Caleb, who was seated beside her now, blew out a long breath as the jury paraded out of the room to deliberate. They each hoped it would be a mercifully speedy decision.

Jon stood and adjusted his jacket. Even in the air-conditioning, the courtroom was uncomfortably warm. "Okay, so we wait."

"It looks good, Jon," his lawyer prompted. "I feel really positive about how today went."

"Thanks, I hope you're right."

Dr. Finley moved in to shake Jon's hand. "Either way, we are delighted to have helped bring about a healthy discussion on the topic of creation science. I am sure it has caused a number of people to reconsider their position on how the earth came to be." He cleared his throat before continuing, "But for your sake, and the sake of your students, I hope to see you teaching again this fall."

Jon smiled his appreciation and shook the man's offered hand.

"Jonnie"—his mother reached out to hug her son—"I'm glad the trial is over. And I agree with Mr. Vollman, I think it went well."

"We'll know soon, I guess."

Esther slipped down beside Jon. "Take a few minutes with your family. The interview can wait. I'll be in the hallway whenever you're ready."

Jon smiled back gratefully. "I won't be long. Thanks."

Esther was pleased that the cameras had been allowed into a side hallway. Here they would have some measure of privacy for an interview with Jon and his family. But Esther knew it would be a very difficult interview. She would need to ask straightforward questions about how the trial had concluded, and she was feeling much more inclined to empathize with them all. A professional air would be difficult to maintain today.

"Welcome, Mr. Shepherd. We're glad you've allowed us to interview you at this sensitive point in the trial. Tell us, how do you feel about the closing remarks?"

"I think they went quite well. I think we were able to state our case clearly and that we were well represented by each of those who gave testimony. I don't see any reason why we shouldn't win today."

"And how about you, Mrs. Shepherd? What was it like for you to watch your son's trial draw to a close?"

Jon's mother, her arm firmly wrapped around Jon's,

leaned forward as she answered. "I don't need to say that this has been a very draining time for us. We're very proud of Jon. He's handled this controversy well. We knew that he would, and no matter what the jury decides, we believe that he acted rightly."

"Thank you, Mrs. Shepherd." Esther smiled back, fighting the feeling of unbidden tears welling up in her eyes.

"Mr. Vollman, what is your reaction, as the defense attorney, to the response of the jury? Did they seem to you to have understood the tremendous amount of scientific discussion and evidence that was presented to them?"

"I believe so, Esther. We made every effort to keep our explanations at a layman's level whenever possible, but there were, admittedly, some witnesses whose testimony was a little difficult for most of us to keep up with."

"Do you think that will prove costly?"

"Not at all. There was overwhelming support given for our side of the case and we have every confidence that the jury will agree."

"Thank you, Mr. Vollman. We certainly wish you the best. Well, there you have it. The unexpectedly lengthy trial of schoolteacher Jon Shepherd has drawn to a close today. The jury has begun deliberations, and it is uncertain just how long it will take to receive a verdict. We'll let you know of any updates as soon as they are available. Back to you, Steve."

Immediately the camera crew began tearing down equipment in order to hustle to another location. Esther herself would not be able to stay long.

"Thanks." Jon had to raise his voice to be heard over the confusion around them.

"You know that when you leave this hallway, you're going to see every crew in town. It's probably better if you make a statement to them today."

"Michael is handling that for us."

"You might want to think about giving your own today.

It makes it easier for people to sympathize with you. Just a suggestion."

"Okay. Maybe."

"How are you doing?"

"I don't know yet." Esther knew it was difficult for Jon to know that there was nothing left to do, nothing left to say. Everything had been taken out of his hands.

"Will you call me tonight?"

"Sure. Or you can probably reach me at the center. There are a whole group of people who are going to wait this thing out with us. I hope they won't be disappointed."

"Just remember, it was decided before it even began."

"I know. And, Esther, thanks for everything you've done to help me—the interviews and all. I know it's been a great help in getting people to understand this whole thing." Then, as if he had preplanned the move, Jon leaned down and kissed Esther softly on the cheek. "Thanks. You've been so . . . just a great . . . well, friend."

He was flustered. Esther was sure he had almost lost his nerve. Had he planned on saying more? She smiled as she watched him begin to blush. Jon had never kissed her before.

Back at the station, Esther rummaged around in her office, forgetting entirely what she had been looking for. She was increasingly fearful that the jury would rule in favor of the school board. She was becoming quite certain that Jon would lose.

"Hi, Esther." Annie had chosen to stay late. "They need you down on set. Did you get your jacket?"

"Oh, right. It's here. Let's go."

Once again, the broadcast seemed to last forever. Esther finally forced herself to stop glancing up at the clock and concentrated instead on the script alone. She knew her performance was weak, but she also knew it could not be helped.

Immediately after the set was pronounced clear, she bolted for her office. Annie was right on her heels.

"Hello? This is Esther Branson. Is Jon handy? May I speak to him please?"

There was an unbearable pause as Jon was sent for.

"Hi."

"Hi, it's Esther."

The restraint in Jon's voice had already given Esther her answer. He was still struggling for the difficult words.

"It's okay, Jon." Esther cradled the phone in both hands. "You can appeal. Michael and Dr. Finley even expected this to happen. It's okay."

"It just takes so long." His voice caught in his throat as he spoke.

"I know. Don't think about that now. Just be glad this round is over. You did very well. And you deserve a rest."

"Yeah, I guess I'll be glad for that."

"I'm going to let you go. You need to be with your family. Call me tomorrow?"

"Sure."

"Good night."

"Good night, Esther. Thanks for calling. I mean it."

"I know," she whispered softly. "Good-bye."

Esther lowered the phone to the desk and looked up at Annie. "He lost."

"I know."

"I don't understand it. They did so well—gave such good testimony."

"I know."

"Oh, Annie. He sounded so down."

Annie slipped an arm around Esther's shoulders and sighed. "You're tired, too, Esther. Let me drive you home."

Esther was too miserable to argue.

❧ ❧ ❧ ❧

"You'd better be . . . more careful, Esther . . . hold the

ball out there . . . like that again . . . and I'll . . . steal it for sure." Jon's words came in short breaths and echoed through the gymnasium.

Esther tucked the basketball in closer to her body and pivoted away from where Jon was standing. Breathless, she lobbed it across to Caleb. If she'd known she'd be out of breath and sweaty she'd have never agreed to be part of this game today. She wasn't even dressed appropriately. No wonder she was doing so poorly.

"All right," she finally conceded, hoping she had played long enough to be considered a good sport. "I'm sure there's someplace else I need to be. Something else I'm supposed to be doing."

"You sure?" Jon seemed to be surprised that she didn't want to continue the game.

"Believe me, I'm sure." Esther retreated to a nearby chair and collapsed onto it.

Jon followed and sat down. "Sorry. I guess we pushed you into playing."

"That's okay. I used to enjoy basketball, but it's been a long time. When I was a kid my best friend Andy and I used to really tear up a court."

Jon smiled. He wasn't really surprised. He had noticed that Esther was still a pretty good shot. "So do you really have to head back to work?"

"Pretty soon."

"Can we talk a minute first?"

"Sure." Esther studied Jon's face. His voice had become serious.

"Let's go out into the hall."

Once settled in a private corner, Jon turned toward Esther and struggled for a way to begin.

"I've decided to appeal." This was not surprising to Esther in the least. She was glad that he had found the courage to do so, but she hoped with all her heart it would not be in vain. "I think it's going to be a pretty bumpy ride."

"I'm afraid I'd have to agree."

Jon tipped his head back a moment thoughtfully. "Since I'm not teaching anymore, I'm going to be doing more work here at the center—full time. And Caleb is going to be heading back to Wisconsin where he's found a job closer to Mom and Dad and Boyd."

"Family is really important to Caleb, isn't it?"

Jon smiled. "It sure is. And I'm really going to miss him being around."

"When will you start the appeal process?"

"Michael said it'll take some time just to get the paper work ready—that I'm looking at at least a couple of months until my case can be reviewed to see if the appeal is justified. I've got to admit, it'll be a relief to think about other things for a while."

"Have you thought about finding another teaching position? Maybe at a Christian school or something?"

"Yeah, I thought about it. But the center can really use my time here, and, well, I really feel like it's more important for me to be with the kids that don't have the good fortune of Christian parents."

Esther smiled. Jon had never really left the mission field. It didn't matter what country he happened to live in.

"I just wanted to tell you how much I've come to appreciate you. I sort of tried to say it after the trial but my words got all twisted. It probably wasn't the right time."

"You had *a lot* on your mind."

"We all did. Anyway, what I wanted to say was that I'd like to get to know you better . . . to take you out . . . to see you more often." He checked himself. "I know you broke off an engagement not long ago and you'll probably want some time to get your own life back together. I'm not wanting to rush you. I'll wait. I just want to say something before I hear you're dating somebody else and I've missed my chance. I know there must be a whole crew of guys standing in line to take you out."

Esther blushed. "Not at all."

"Well, once the word is out that you're free, there will be. I just want you to know that I'm interested if you are."

"I won't forget."

With an awkwardness that both of them shared, Esther smiled a warm response and excused herself to leave for work. Walking out the door of the youth center and into the sunshine, Esther blushed again. He had spoken as if he believed she would be doing him a favor by allowing him to date her. How could she make him understand that she felt just the opposite? That Jon was, himself, a prize—one that she wasn't sure she deserved.

But it seemed they would have plenty of opportunity ahead to convince each other.

# Twenty-two

*Friday, December 31*

Esther forced her head to pass through the shimmering folds of blueness, let them fall with a rustling sound around her shoulders, and shook them gently until the hem of the dress swept against the floor. The coolness of the evening gown, the shivers it sent up her spine to see her reflection in the mirror, the anticipation that almost burst from her as she thought about the evening ahead—Esther wanted to savor every moment, every sensation of this incredible night.

For weeks now, the city—no, the whole country, perhaps even the world—had seemed to throb with excitement in anticipation of welcoming the beginning of a new century. Every newscast had counted down the days, replayed highlights of the *old* century that was being left behind, and given projections about what might change and what would prove to be timeless. Special celebrations in each city around the nation had begun to be in the news as early as the autumn colors had fallen. With a new president ready to take office and hopes high for the economy and world affairs, Esther was indeed swept along in the excitement, both while reading the news at the station and in her personal life. She and Jon had found many ways to enjoy each other's company in the months that had passed.

And more recently, Esther had just returned from a glorious week in Nebraska. Her mother and she had enjoyed each other with an abandon they had not experienced in years. Shopping and baking and going to movies, they felt carefree and relaxed, enjoying every moment together.

It had been wonderful to be with Granddad again, too. Esther spent as much time as she was able talking with him and making him comfortable during his stay at her mother's house. She had missed him every bit as much as she had expected she would.

All too soon, Esther had needed to return to Atlanta to take her part in the New Year's celebration which had really begun in earnest the day after Christmas. This evening's party would be the culmination of it all, and Esther was breathless with anticipation.

Soon Jon would arrive in a limousine, much like Prince Charming in his carriage, to escort her to the gala event. He had agreed to wear a tuxedo for the first time in his life, and Esther had pictured him time and again standing on the porch step in the twilight, waiting to sweep her away.

Suddenly, she heard his knock at the door. It was time. Breezing down the hallway, Esther stopped as a sudden inspiration hit her. She had to see him before he saw her. With stealthy movements, Esther lifted the curtain on the window beside the apartment door and peeked out to where Jon was standing. His back was turned to her. He would never know that she was spying on him.

Her eyes passed over the smooth lines of the tuxedo across his shoulders. She saw his arm come up as he checked his watch and then passed his fingers through his hair. With girlish delight, Esther watched as he turned toward the door to knock a second time.

But the expression on his face was not as she had envisioned, and a giggle fought to escape her throat. There he was, standing so awkwardly in his tuxedo and bow tie, pulling at the collar as if he wished it could be loosened. The fairytale feeling that had descended over her earlier along with her dress seemed to evaporate as she smiled toward him. She should be feeling nothing but excitement and love, but instead she was ashamed to find herself rather amused.

With no more hesitation, Esther flung open the door.

This time it was Jon who was breathless. "You look incredible," he whispered.

Now that she was near him, close enough to see the look in his eyes, Esther's heart began to race. She was reminded again that Jon was to her much more than a fluttery feeling and a reason to blush. He was her hero in so many ways. He was her ally and her new best friend. He was so gentle and honest and kind. He had accepted her fully, in spite of her struggles over what she wanted most in life. He had taken her for who she was. She would be grateful to do the same.

"Are you ready to go?" he asked tensely.

"Yes. Are you?"

"Oh, I don't think so. I hope I don't embarrass you terribly. I feel like I'm dressed for a costume party. Do I look as ridiculous as I feel?"

Esther leaned forward to kiss him softly. "You look wonderful."

Together they walked to the waiting limousine and Esther bundled her skirt to climb inside. Once settled, she leaned closer to Jon and took his arm.

"I feel so full of emotion I could burst. In my head I know that tomorrow morning will be just another day, but I can't get my heart to calm down."

"My heart is racing, too, Esther." Jon's voice was rich and full. The sound of it brought Esther's eyes up to meet his. "I want to ask you a question. I hope it's the right time."

Esther's heart stopped.

"I love you, Esther. Not just because you're charming and beautiful and strong. But also because I realized a month or so ago that I don't want to be without you, *ever*. That I want to spend every day with you. That I need to be near you. Will you marry me?"

"Oh yes. I will." Her words were almost inaudible, but her eyes looking into Jon's were filled with the things she was telling him.

"For better or for worse?" Esther knew what Jon meant. The appeal process was still ongoing. As the New Year broke, there could easily be—would surely be—difficult days ahead. Was she ready? Was she willing to commit to sharing all of those difficult times with Jon?

"For better or for worse," Esther repeated back meaningfully. He understood. She was certain he did. His ring was sliding over her finger. It was resting in the place where Neal's ring had been. Esther looked down toward it. It was not as expensive as Neal's had been, but Esther loved it so much more—would cherish it every day she was given to share with this man. She turned her eyes back up to meet Jon's.

"I love you," he whispered, leaning closer and kissing her tenderly.

What would the New Year hold for them? There were no guarantees—no way to plan for what would happen or guard against what might be. But walking beside Jon, joining the crowds of people who were sharing in the celebration of the New Year, Esther was ready. As difficult as the road to this moment had been, she would not have chosen to change any of it. God had truly worked all things together for good.

# A Word From the Author

The movement toward scientific study of creation is very real, although each of the characters and the research association mentioned in this book are entirely fictional. I wanted to take this opportunity to recommend further reading for anyone interested in knowing more than the brief summary of facts and ideas presented in this novel. I am pleased to list the following two books as being most helpful to me in my research and also most enjoyable to my family. But there are many more wonderful books to be found, and the children and parents of today can be much better educated on the subject of origins than when I was a child.

*It Couldn't Just Happen*, by Lawrence O. Richards (Word Publishing, 1989), is an excellent book for helping kids become aware of how reasonable their faith in a Creator is and in presenting to them in a visually interesting format just how much the Theory of Evolution falls short of proving itself. My own son said, "It really strengthened my faith." Excellent testimony from an eleven-year-old.

*In the Beginning: Compelling Evidence for Creation and the Flood*, by Walt Brown (Center for Scientific Creation, 1995), is a thorough and eye-opening journey for adults. I was amazed and excited by what was presented in this book and very grateful for all of the work that went into the publication of it. If you're interested in delving deeply into the scientific theory of creation, this is an excellent source for you.